Father, Creator, Spirit -

Verndari Reckoning

by

Deborah Lamoreaux

E

ISBN:978-1-968792-17-6

PROLOGUE

Like being hypnotized, Jake stared at the large spinning wheel right above him.

The only thing he could see, it lit up with rapid flashes. Random images of objects, geometric shapes, animals, people he didn't know, odd-looking ancient concrete structures, even food, and last of all, numbers.

He had a vague recollection of going to bed, and an even more nebulous sense that somehow, he was still in it. But beyond that…

Nothing.

10…9…8…7. In his mind he followed the countdown. Felt drowsy, even foggy, as an unusual and unnerving sensation of disconnection settled upon him…

3…2…1…

Time's up…

Someone or something tugged on his ankles, but from inside his feet. By pure instinct, he threw his arms back over his head, grasped the sturdy pole on the top left of his four-poster bed, the side on which he always slept.

"What in the actual–"

No sooner had the bad word entered his brain than he began to fight in earnest against whatever was attempting to pull him right out of his body. How was this even possible? He couldn't see a thing, surrounded by an oppressive pitch blackness as he was, but there was no mistaking the feeling. Unlike anything he'd ever experienced in his life before. He didn't know how, but he knew…it was without a doubt the separation of his soul from his physical body.

SNAP!

He awoke to his harsh, gasping breaths and looked down at blurry, whitened knuckles.

His hands, no longer latched onto his bedpost, were instead gripping the edges of…

Something…

He fought to make his eyes focus.

"The flowers… They're beautiful. Aren't they?"

His head spun to the left, in the direction of the soft words.

"Hard to believe…but this park has had the largest and most spectacular assortment of tulips in all of the Netherlands, and even the world, for nearly two centuries."

A man.

Dressed all in white robes. He came into crisp relief. Early thirties, if Jake had to guess. And sitting right across from him on…he looked around and down again at what he'd been gripping for the last couple seconds. The edges of a wooden bench, by the looks of it.

He relaxed his hold and turned to his left again.

"I'm sorry…what'd you say?"

A warm smile and eyes filled with such compassion held his gaze.

"These are the Keukenhof Gardens. The park we're sitting in," the stranger gestured with a casual hand. "I think you might enjoy seeing it."

"You think I–?"

"There'll be time enough for questions later. There are always more questions. Trust me. Why not take a moment to enjoy the view instead?" He turned away and gazed out at the gardens in front of them.

Lulled by his calm manner and soothing tone, without another thought, he did what the stranger recommended.

"There you go. Don't you feel better?"

And surprisingly…he did.

All around him, for as far as he could see, there were flowers of every hue and description. A truly amazing and heaven-sent assortment. Filling every square inch of his vision. Reaching out to connect with him in a way he couldn't begin to comprehend or explain.

"Now, take a deep breath in. Let it all become a part of you. That's it. Just inhale the sweet fragrance. Feel that soft dirt under your feet."

He dug his bare toes into the cool, rich soil. Looked down and felt a jolt of joy like no other.

He looked up again, out at the sea of sheer, unadulterated beauty, and then to the left…into the eyes of a friend.

They shared a smile.

He looked out again, at the gorgeous view, and then opened his eyes, by slow degrees. Even as his senses clung to the lingering smell of fragrant flowers, the feel of the soft soil beneath his feet, and visual flashes of extraordinary natural beauty. All elements of his recent experience filled his thoughts, capturing his mind like nothing he'd ever known. For a few moments more. At least until the familiar items in his room, one by one, came into sharp focus in the harsh light of day. All but obliterating the last fragments of his recent sensory excursion.

He swung his legs off his bed and rubbed a hand across his face. That was for sure the freakiest dream he'd ever had. So intense were the lows, but more especially, the highs.

A lingering feeling of such comfort and peace surrounded and clung to him.

Along with a vague recollection of the value of simple things.

For right there at his feet had surely been the prettiest, most exquisite little lily he'd ever seen in his entire life.

Chapter 1

Luke 12:27
Consider the lilies how they grow: they toil not, they spin not; and yet I say unto you, that Solomon in all his glory was not arrayed like one of these...

"Oh, hello Melly," she tapped the side of her glasses as a call came through.

"Hey girl! Haven't heard from you in ages. You would not believe how much I've missed our little calls. Talk about the value of simple things. You always share the timeliest words of wisdom. So thought I'd give you a call to touch base, in case you need to hear some from me. What's going on with you?"

"Yes. It's been a while. Hasn't it? I've been kind of busy, but I'm fine. It's great to hear from you though. How have you been?"

"I am blessed. Just landed this new job with an up-and-coming non-profit. I'm creating all sorts of new content. Working practically twelve-hour days, but hey, I am loving every minute of it!"

"Oh, good. That's so great. Glad to hear it."

"So, what about you? How are things in California? Getting any closer to tenure?"

"Me? Oh no, I left my job, and Cali, a while ago. Felt like a fresh start."

"You're kidding? Where are you now?"

"Here, in NYC."

"Really? I can't believe you're right here in my home state. And you haven't even reached out? What gives?"

"Oh, I left in a bit of a rush, so I'm still settling in. The opportunity came up at precisely the time I needed it. You know how that can be."

"Oh, yeah sure. That's so cool though. But wait…what about Stuart?"

"Him…? Uh…no. It didn't work out." She tried a dry laugh.

"But he was so gorgeous though. What happened?"

"Yes, well looks can certainly be deceiving. He might have looked like the black Adonis of my dreams, but he turned out to be far from it. Trust me. Guess that's what I get for yoking myself to someone of unequal faith, right? Had me convinced he was different. That he wanted me to lead him to the Lord. What a joke. What he actually wanted was to wear me down and lead me to his bed, but I wasn't having it. He finally got tired of waiting I guess, and couldn't keep up the pretense any longer."

"Now why would you say that?"

"Because the last time we spoke, months ago, he took great pleasure in letting me know exactly how many women he'd been with while he was quote-unquote, killing time waiting on me."

"Unbelievable. What an A-class jerk!"

"You're telling me."

"Well, I say good riddance then. You can do so much better than that loser."

"Absolutely. I know that's right."

She kept her verbal chin up for her friend's benefit, but inside for a minute, she was that young woman again, wondering when she, just her, the person she truly was, would ever be enough, for anyone. She stifled a sigh.

"It's so weird, now that I think about it, I thought I saw him, the other day when I got into work. I was headed upstairs to my floor and I caught a glimpse of this homeless guy heading into the shelter in the line for breakfast. It was so freaky how much he looked like him. Could have been his twin brother. You know what they say, everyone's got a doppelganger out in the world somewhere, I guess."

"Yes, that is what they say. Listen, Melly. I'm picking up a couple things at the store at the moment, so can I ring you back later?"

"Oh, yeah. Sure. I'm holding you to that by the way. Don't disappear on me again. Promise?"

"No, of course I won't."

"You need to send me your new address and stuff too, don't forget."

"Yes, of course I will. Thanks so much for checking in. You stay blessed and take care."

"You, too. We'll get together soon."

"Yes. Okay, bye."

She rubbed a hand across her forehead as she relived an unpleasant memory for the hundredth time at least.

"So, you know anything about broccoli?"

Her gaze snapped up as she tapped her glasses to end the call. There, across the floating produce table, she locked gazes with a pair of the brightest blue eyes she'd ever seen. Right above a slightly crooked nose and a pair of nice-looking male lips. Early forties, if she had to guess. He was quite attractive when you put his different facial features together. Went pretty well with his salt and pepper hair and big, but somehow still lean, six-foot-plus frame, too.

She remembered he'd asked her a question. About broccoli, was it?

"I'm sorry, did you say something?"

His head tipped to the side as he smiled.

Oh, so there was a fantastic smile to go along with that good-looking face.

"Yes, I was asking if you knew how to pick out some top-tier broccoli. Other than the fact that it's definitely bad once it's yellow, or gone all dark and moldy, I never know which heads are the best." He waved a hand over the staggering selection on one of the trays between them, to his left and her right.

"Oh, no. Sorry," she shook her head. "Not really my cup of tea. The brightest green maybe? I'm afraid I'm much more of a fresh salad kind of girl."

"Oh? Is that right?"

"Yes, and fruit. You want to talk about how to select the best strawberries and cherries, well, then I'm your girl."

"Good to know. So—"

She heard a 'she's gotta have it' ring tone emanating from somewhere on his person.

Unbelievable…

"Uh, I'm so sorry. I need to take this. Don't go away, please? Just give me one minute."

He held up an index finger then flipped his shades down from atop his head. Tapped the side of them.

"Hey, Sam. Now's not a good time. Besides, aren't we seeing each other tonight? Is something wrong?"

"What? What do you mean, you're spending the weekend down the coast? With who...? A group of your friends? Which friends...? Oh, I know exactly how old you are. Don't play with me young lady. Be specific. I want names, because it better not be with any of those sketchy girls I told you to stop hanging out with. Yes... Okay... I remember her. Yes... Wait, did you say Garrett? You mean the same Garrett you cried your eyes out over, a month ago? Samantha Elizabeth Traynor... Yes, here we go. And why shouldn't I call you that? It's your name, isn't it? Do you mean the same guy you broke up with, and had me going to the store to get you ice cream like your mom used to do, to cheer you up? And at 1 AM in the morning? That Garrett?! Okay, okay... No, I'm calm. I'm calm. See? This is me, being calm...It's just I thought you were done with that boy, honey."

Facing him across the produce table, she wondered if she should give him some privacy and move away. Although he *had* asked her to stay. Plus, when had she ever been polite when she knew she could help. Sounded like he was about to get into it with his trouble-prone-teen-aged daughter. As discretely as she could, she reached into her pocket, pulled out her intuitive 'thoughts to text' disc, and stuck her fingers under her hair so she could set it to her temple.

"Ask her why she wants to go," she said in her mind and then held up her hand to him where she knew his daughter wouldn't be able to see the screen text rising out of the coms, the communication data dots, at her wrist.

She waved her hand around, till he finally noticed it and read her text. He did a double take.

"Excuse me?"

"Ask her why she wants to go. Trust me," she gave him a pointed look as she held her hand up a bit closer for him to read her last thought.

"Uh… no, not you, honey." He looked like he wasn't going to take her advice, but then he relented.

"So, tell me…why do you even want to go spend an entire weekend with Garrett? Especially given what happened last time you two hung out."

He listened to her response.

"So, let me get this straight," he looked across at her, "you think this ex of his poisoned him against you before?"

He gave a shrug of futility.

"So, he's still close enough to this ex of his that he'd take what she says over what he knows about her?"

He gave her a thumbs-up sign and mouthed, "Good one."

"So, don't you think it's a red flag that he's listening to whatever random thing his ex has to say, instead of talking to you…? Okay, and if they're still thick as thieves, you need to consider what that means for you, don't you?"

"Ask her if the ex-girlfriend is going down the coast too."

"So, what about this ex of his? Is she going on this trip too? She is, huh?"

"Ask her if she feels comfortable being put in a position where she'll feel like she has to compete."

"So, are you comfortable being put in a position like that? I mean, won't you feel like the two of you are in competition for his attention the entire time you're there? Uh-huh…yes, I'll bet you didn't think of it that way."

"He's happy to eat his cake and keep it too I'll bet, so ask her if she wouldn't prefer to know if he'd choose her."

"Wouldn't it be better to remove yourself from the equation? See if he'll miss you? Don't you want to know if he'd choose you when he's faced with that choice?

"BTW, just out of curiosity, this isn't about an S.E.X. thing, too, is it? Oh, thank God." He put a hand up to his forehead. "What? I had to ask. You never know these days. You kids are growing up so fast.

"So, you'll sit out this trip and think about it some more? Really? Okay, well, I'm so glad I could help too. You're welcome and I…I love you, too, honey." The hand at his head moved to his chest.

"Yes. I'll see you later for dinner at the house. Okay, bye."

He tapped the side of his glasses and turned to her. A huge heart-melting smile wreathed his face.

"You know, since my ex-wife and I split, I've been struggling to establish some kind of connection with Sam…uh, that was my daughter by the way."

"I figured," she nodded.

"To be honest, I'd be happy to see the back of that guy. He's not good enough for her. What if he's trying to…you know…get in her pants?"

"Well, if he's toying with her and he wants the ex, instead, then he probably won't pursue it any further since she didn't take the bait. If he does care about her then he'll miss her, and maybe choose her and let her know it. Either way. It's a win-win."

"And thanks to you I think I may have made some real progress today. That's the first time she's said 'I love you' to me in years. I can't thank you enough."

"No problem. But I should tell you, I absolutely draw the line at having 'the S.E.X. talk'. So, you're on your own with that one my friend."

"Duly noted," he chuckled.

"Oh, and I'd change that ringtone if I were you. Not appropriate in the least."

"That's because you don't know my daughter. Ever since she could talk. From two years old it's been 'Dad, can I have this? Dad, can you please get me that?' I swear she thinks I'm an ATM, or Santa Clause, or something." He chuckled.

"Oh, okay. I see what you're saying."

"Right? Trust me, it's perfect for her."

"You think so? I'm curious though…have you ever listened to the entire song? Not just the chorus that's used for the ringtone? Or ever seen the video that goes along with it?"

"No, why?"

"Well," she hit a few of the colorful data dots on her wrist, made a selection from the list of songs that came up, then held her palm out to where he could easily see it. "You might want to take a look at this."

Almost from the outset, a couple of scantily clad young women filled the space above her hand and began a booty shaking extravaganza. And they were not to be outdone by their male counterparts, in what soon escalated into a sex-with-clothes-on, live in 3-D simulation.

"Oh…crap. Are you serious? Don't…please. Don't. Show me anymore." His face turned pale then beet red.

He held his wrist up near to his mouth.

"Change Sam's ringtone. NOW."

"Please make a selection from the following options."

"Anything. Generic."

"I'm sorry, but that is not one of the available options. Please make another selection from the listed menu."

"Uh…please go back to the manufacturer's default then."

"Resetting all phone settings to manufacturer's preset."

"What? No! Stop. Uhm, abort. Only the ringtone for that number."

She felt a giggle bubble up at the discomfited expression on his face, but she suppressed it.

A plain bell tone sounded. "Ringtone changed."

"Oh, thank God," he clutched his chest, "and thank *you*. You are a life saver. Yuh know that?"

She snorted and the giggle she'd tried to restrain escaped her lips. She put the back of her hand up to her mouth.

"I'm sorry, but do you think this is somehow funny?" He looked mildly perturbed at first, but then the left side of his mouth quirked upward. "Okay, I guess it was kinda funny."

"Are you kidding me? It's hilarious! You should have seen the expression on your face when you thought your phone was resetting. And when you saw that video? It was priceless. You've never seen it before?"

"Obviously not. Go ahead. Laugh it up. You must think I'm the poster-boy for those goofy dad jokes people tell."

"The thought did cross my mind. I mean, 'she's gotta have it?' That title? It didn't strike you as being even a teensy bit risqué when you saw it in the list of tones?"

"No. I promise you. That? Whatever that was in the video? Never crossed my girl-dad mind. Not in a million years."

"I'll bet." She started laughing again and this time he joined her for a few moments.

"You know, you look familiar," he said, as he sobered.

"Yes... I was thinking the same thing about you too."

"I've seen you on the campus of Sunnyvale University where I teach, haven't I?"

"Oh, of course, now that you mention it, I think I've probably seen you crossing the quad."

"Yes, that's right. Are you a student?"

"You're kidding me, right? Do I look young enough to be a student?"

"Hey, I know way better than to ask, or answer, any age-related question when it comes to the ladies, so next question, please."

She chuckled. "As it happens, I'm a professor. Of English lit."

"Oh really?" His brows rose as his smile brightened. "That's wonderful. It also explains your perfect diction. Are you from England?"

"Me? Oh no. My father is though. But I don't think I sound British. Surely not. Do I?"

"No, you're right. Not British exactly. Maybe British adjacent? You don't actually have any accent I can place, but there's something about the way you speak… Like the way you said straw-breeze, instead of straw-berries. I liked that. It's subtle. Cultured. Classy."

"Why, thank you. I'll take that as a compliment."

"Yes…you should…"

His head angled to the side again, his lips lifting in that slow smile she was beginning to enjoy.

"I can't believe I haven't seen you at any faculty meetings yet."

"Well, we're a big group, plus, I recently transferred in from California. Just last month actually."

"Oh, that explains it. I teach philosophy and political science. Jake Traynor." He extended his hand.

"Scout Kavanagh, but everyone calls me Lily." She shook it. Tried to let go and couldn't.

"Excuse me?" His eyes widened, his gaze piercing as he shook her hand, then held it for long seconds.

"I know, right? Lily is as far away from Scout as you could get. But there it is. It's my mum's favorite flower, which is odd because she's from the Caribbean. But, I'm an only child, so…" In her mind, she scolded herself for rambling, probably like an idiot. Closed her mouth and smiled. Concentrated on extricating her hand from his warm grasp without snatching it away.

"So… Scout? Really?" He cleared his throat and stared.

She knew her given name was unusual. Did he have to make it so obvious exactly how odd he considered it to be? If he was older, she'd have been summoning a holo-doc right then, given how shook-up he looked.

"Yes…what can I say? My parents were big…I mean just huge *To Kill a Mockingbird* fans."

"Oh, right." He shook his head as though clearing it of something. "I think I remember being forced to read that for some kind of extra-curricular book report in undergrad years ago."

"Forced?" She chuckled. "One is not coerced into reading vintage Harper Lee, or any of the literary ultra-classics for that matter, Mr. Traynor. It is instead a bona fide privilege. One you should grasp with eager, open hands."

"A privilege, huh?"

His crooked little grin was contagious.

She nodded, then stifled a little giggle as she tried to look serious.

"Well, let's agree to disagree on that score, Professor. Oh, and call me Jake, please. You've literally just had a ringside seat for me reliving most of my dubious dating experience right up until senior prom, in one single conversation with my daughter. Not to mention the whole, she's gotta shake her booty for all the boys, ringtone fiasco. I feel like you're one of my dearest friends already. Or at the very least, my psychologist," he grinned.

"Sure, Jake. And you can call me Lily."

"Not Scout?"

"Not if you'd like to keep breathing."

He barked out a laugh. "Oh, trust me, I would."

He paused…looked at her.

"So… Lily it will be…

"…So beautiful…it's such a beautiful name, I mean."

"Why thank you Jake. You're not so bad yourself."

She smiled as he chuckled.

"Okay, well I've gotta run." She dragged her gaze away and looked at her watch. "I've actually got to teach a class in half an hour."

"Yes, sure." He smiled.

"It was so wonderful meeting you. I've made friends with so few people here so far. It's wonderful to know there'll be a familiar face nearby on campus."

"Same here. And here's all my info." He tapped his glasses, and she got a proximity alert on hers. "Call me anytime. Oh, and thanks again for the relationship counselling and everything. I meant what I said. I really appreciated it."

"Sure, any time. Here's mine." She sent him her number and email.

"Maybe you'll let me take you out to dinner sometime this week? To say a proper thank you?" He eyed her with a hopeful little smile.

Wait… What?

When did they take the leap from harmless flirtation not amounting to anything, straight to a 'let's make this happen' dinner invite?

"Uh…we'll see. Well… okay. Hope you enjoy your weekend."

"Well… okay then?" His expression and tone faltered straight from hesitant into vague confusion, and she wondered if her response had been a bit too abrupt.

Darn it, Lily, there you go. Scare off one of the few friends you've made in this place so far, why don't you?

She held her breath.

But then he smiled again, and she released it, gratefully.

"Thanks… Uh… You have a good one too. Okay, well, you take care now."

He hesitated, then turned and headed in the direction of the checkout with his basket of groceries.

"Oh, wait. Jake?!"

He spun back. "Yes?"

"You, uh, you forgot to get your broccoli."

"No… No, I didn't actually. Can't stand it. I'm much more of a potato chips kinda guy." His smile was lazy and full of supreme male confidence.

She gasped. "Okay. So, it's like that? I see you!" She grinned then wagged a finger at him.

"I hoped you would. See *you* around, Lily." He winked.

"You wish, Professor." She barked out a laugh, then shook her head as she turned on her heel and headed in the opposite direction.

Chapter 2

Proverbs 1:5
A wise man will hear, and will increase learning; and a
man of understanding shall attain unto wise counsels...

"So, you folks see me...in this class nearly every week, right?" Lily leaned back against her desk at the front of the large room. "What would you say if I just walked in here one day and told you to hand me the smart keys to your car? And–"

"I'd say take it, with my most esteemed compliments, Ms. Kavanagh," a male British-accented voice called out from the back of the tiered seating and was promptly rewarded with a round of boisterous laughter from around the room.

"At which point I'd say, I'll pass. Absolutely *no one* needs, or wants, that piece of crap you call transport, Bradford, but thank you. Am I right, people?"

To which she received a chorus of verbal agreement, laughter and clapping. While Brad got a few slaps on the back from those nearby, and some e-graphic missiles launched in his direction from some of those who were further away.

"Oh, good one Katy!" Lily grinned. "That exploding e-bomb that throws literal shade on the intended target was inspired. I've never seen anything like it."

"Oh, it's the Rizz Bossiest, Ms. Kavanagh. I'll be sure to proxim it to you," a pretty brunette near the front looked back at the object of her assault, then giggled as he blew her a kiss. She spun back and tapped the data dots on her wrist.

Right away, Lily got the silent proximity alert on her glasses. "Thank you so much. I'll be sure to use this." She saved the communication from Katy.

"Okay, so as I was saying, provided you'll allow me to continue with my rhetorical questions, Brad…" She grinned, and another couple of bubbles of laughter popped up around the room, but softer this time. "What if I also said to you that if you don't give me your keys, I'll make sure you fail my class this semester? Plus, I'll see to it that the Dean of Administration learns that you're a complete slacker, and cuts you from the roster entirely this year, hmm? Now…question for real, tell me, what would you call behavior like that?"

"Mean." Someone called out.

"Yes, sure, and what else?"

"An abuse of power?"

"Yes, absolutely, Luke. Very good! And more specifically? Come on… I'm looking for one word… What's the noun you'd ascribe to an abuse of power?"

"Manipulation?"

"Precisely, Andy. Good job! Manipulation. It happens to be one of the main themes we're going to be focusing on next, as we study one of Shakespeare's most acclaimed tragedies, Macbeth. It explores in depth the dangers of manipulation, unchecked ambition, the corrupting influence of power and greed, moral decay, and even the debilitating effects of guilt."

She read out a couple pertinent segments of the play for their edification and then laid out the assignment for the next session.

"Okay, people, so I expect you to read at least the first Act, write a summary of the scenes, and also an analysis highlighting prime examples of the main themes you notice, as I've articulated them. Of course, as usual, please come prepared to discuss when next we meet. Macbeth can be pretty heavy stuff, so we want the sessions to be as interactive and as engaging as we can make them. Yes?"

The end-of-session alert sounded all around the room.

"Right, class dismissed. Off you go! And no googling, and absolutely no AI assistance, I'll know," she pointed an accusing finger in several directions as they started to rise to leave.

"Bloody hell, Ms. Kavanagh." Brad called out again from the back. "I say, that list of deliverables is positively diabolical. Couldn't I just give you my car after all?"

She shook her head with a grin as the room erupted with fresh laughter.

Chapter 3

2 Corinthians 6:9
As unknown, and yet well known; as dying, and, behold,
we live; as chastened, and not killed...

Lily opened her eyes to a large, dimly lit room.

Sparse furnishings, looking dodgy at best, were scattered in a haphazard manner around the space. Including a couple chairs, a threadbare couch, and… a car?

In one sweeping glance, she took in the vehicle in which she was sitting. The laser-enhanced windshield and windows, the reinforced doors, the racing car steering wheel, the plush interior, and the high-tech instrumentation panel with all its gadgets and gizmos.

And to her left…a somewhat familiar, if blurry face turned in her direction, but asleep, by the looks of him.

"Jake?"

She tried to speak his name and couldn't. Heard an eerie echo in her head instead, which in turn alerted her to exactly where she was.

She touched his arm, gave it a gentle shake.

He jerked awake. Looked at her and around. His mouth started moving but emitted no sound.

"I know this feels strange, but just try to relax. It will help you use your mind to communicate." She touched his hand. He grasped it. Held on tight, as she nodded at him in reassurance. *"That's it… Focus on your breaths."* She heard the sound of his labored breathing slow, by degrees.

"Woah… this is so weird, how well I can understand you." He looked at her, his expression still stunned. *"This is amazing."* The deep, pleasant tone of his voice flowed around in her brain, yet still odd, as it mingled with her thoughts.

He looked down at their joined hands. Released his hold with a slow stroking caress right to her fingertips.

Shocked at how good his touch felt, she curled her fingernails into her palms in her lap. Normally pleasurable sensations of touch, smell, and taste, were dull in the void. But that was anything but. Which left her to wonder…

What might it be like to be touched by him…in that manner, back in the real world?

No one. No man, had touched her like that since Stuart. And with him, she'd come to realize, at great cost, it had always been a preamble to a calculated attempt to elicit more from her.

With him a kiss was never just a kiss. Never a mere demonstration of affection. A touch, never a gesture of connection. Instead, they were all carefully orchestrated maneuvers, in his war of seduction. All designed to deceive and manipulate her into giving her body to him. To someone who didn't even know for instance that she preferred tea over coffee, wonderful rhythmic Trinidad Soca rather than pop music, and trips to the opera instead of flying car shows. But then why would he? She'd done everything he wanted to do from the minute she met him. Suppressed her own wants and preferences. Acquiesced to his, at every turn. All so he'd like her and want to spend time with her, so she wouldn't have to be alone.

She looked over at the man beside her. Watched as he flexed his fingers, on both hands. As he touched his hair, his face, and his chest. He looked down, pressed a button on the driver side panel and watched as the door to the car rose up and out like the sleek wing of an eagle. He swung his legs out, put his feet down on the carpet on the floor outside the car, wiggled his toes a bit, then pulled his legs inside again.

He closed the door and then turned to her and smiled.

"Well, hi there. Welcome back," she gave him a quirky smile of her own.

"This... Is amazing," he said again. Looked out the front windscreen, then did a double take.

She watched his smile fade and his eyes widen after two heads with connected shoulders popped in through the far wall ahead of them, looked around and then went back out just as fast.

"Oh, dear God. Did you see that? Those people? Wait, was that two, or one? They were..."

"Yes, that's kind of how this all works. Freaky, huh?"

"You're telling me. I've never seen anything like that. And us? This is like some kind of weird shared dream. Only uh...darker, more like a nightmare maybe." He looked back over at the far wall.

"You have no idea."

"Nice car though..." He grasped the steering wheel in front of him with near reverence. Then touched the instrument panel directly below the windscreen as though it was something he did every day. The engine thrummed into powerful, rumbling life. *"Very nice."* He murmured.

Wasn't that just like a man?

So obviously terrified of his surroundings in one moment, to the exclusion of all else, and then completely enamored with a flashy car in the very next.

"Yes, it is, isn't it?"

Odd, but come to think of it, she hadn't even pictured a car like this one during her class.

"Look, I won't pretend to know why we're here, together, but I do feel like I should probably come clean. You likely have me to thank for this vehicle. I'm afraid I was thinking and even talking about a car during one of my classes today. Similar to dreams, things in here tend to mirror whatever we've experienced. Or even what we've wished for in the past. Though rarely in a good way, and never for long."

"So, you've been here...wherever this is, before?" He switched off the engine and angled his big body to face her, in the cramped space.

"Well, not this place specifically." She glanced around, keeping her eye out for the changes she could

sense, more than see, beginning to happen in the room all around them. *"But yes, I've been in the void far too many times to count. You? Your first time, I'm guessing?"*

"It's strange, I feel like I've been once before…maybe, I think. Or at least I started to… Hmm…the void… You know, you said that name and I knew exactly what you meant. Almost as though I've heard it before."

"Yes, I had that same feeling too when the word sort of popped into my head the first time. It fits though, doesn't it?"

"Yes, that's definitely how I'd describe this place. It's strange…I can see the things and the people that came into the room. Even this car, but somehow it feels…I don't know…empty somehow?"

"Yes, and I know it's very scary in here sometimes, between the lost souls and the fallen angels, but each time I encounter another living soul like us, I like to think that this way of communicating like we are right now, is simply the Lord's way of showing us at least a little bit of heaven in the midst of all this hell."

"Hmm, interesting perspective. So, what do you think? What should we do now?"

"No clue."

"Huh? But you just said you've been here lots of times. Shouldn't you be sharing a brilliant plan of action? Or some timely wisdom at the very least?"

"What? You mean other than we should exit with all haste, before the room fills with more of them?" She waved a hand towards the truly freakazoid assortment of looky-loos that had already gathered,

and were still coming in through the walls, ceiling, and floor, and starting to congregate in corners of the room.

"Them? Them who?" He glanced around then turned back to her, looking confused.

"Those ones over there… Wait…you don't see them?"

He looked back to where she'd pointed.

"What the–?!"

She heard the expletive he uttered next, detonate in her brain like a grenade.

"Language!" She glared at him, *"but yes, that about covers it."*

"Sorry. That slipped out. But dang… Who are they? Lost souls, or the fallen you mentioned?"

"Best guess? I'd say the lost. See that lot over there?" She indicated a group in a corner talking and gesticulating. *"They're looking over here every now and again, but they're mostly talking amongst themselves. Granted, it can be quite unpleasant when they gang up on you, but it takes them a while to get organized. The fallen have a way of zeroing in on you the second they see you. Like with laser focus.*

"Also, see how their feet are actually touching the floor?"

He nodded.

"The fallen angels never quite seem to connect with the ground. It's as though they've never had to walk before, you know? They sort of hover, I guess is the best way to describe it. That's why I don't think it's them. Well, that and the fact that by now they would most certainly have already tried to attack us."

"Wow, so that was ten parts insightful and ninety parts freaky. Like I really wish you'd never said that because you literally blew my mind, kind of freaky."

"Sorry, but you asked."

"Yes, I did. Well, whichever they are, I think we need to get out of here."

"I would concur."

"Look. Over there. Ask and you shall receive," he pointed to the right of them to where an antique wooden door in the wall had just opened up onto a busy street. Set slightly ajar, bright daylight filtered in, in beckoning invitation.

"Let's go that way. What if I put on the front bumper deflectors, floor the gas, and we drive straight through it? Are you with me?"

"Hmm..." she started to give it some thought, but apparently impatient for her response, he hit the starter on the car. It made a sick little choking sound, then died. He tried it again, three more times, with the same disappointing result.

"Unbelievable," he hit the instrumentation panel once with the palm of his hand.

"Oh dear, I fear that won't work either. I rather doubt that you'll be able to thrash it into submission." She grinned at his pointless effort.

He graced her with an incredulous look.

*"Also, that is precisely what I was afraid would happen. The one thing you'll learn is that this place is consistent in one way: things **never** go the way you imagine."*

"Okay, so plan B then. If we can't drive through it, I say we make a run for the door instead."

"I'm not so sure…" she looked up through the car's sunroof and gauged the distance to the ceiling high overhead.

"What? Do you have a better idea than us getting the heck out of Lucifer's Lamborghini right now?"

"Seriously?" She felt a quite inappropriate giggle bubble up. She suppressed it and eyed him instead. *"Did you have to say that name?"*

"Hey, I call it like I see it. Besides, he's not Beetlejuice.*"* His lips quirked upward. *"It's not like he'll appear at the sound of his name, or anything. Wait…he won't, will he?"* His face fell.

"Again, contrary to popular belief, I haven't the foggiest, so let's not chance it, shall we?"

"Okay, so what? You think we should try to wait it out in here? Lock the windows and the doors. See if they'll leave?"

"They won't leave. In my experience, even more will come. Oh, and FYI, the doors and windows, in fact the entire structure of this car is nothing but an elaborate illusion."

She leaned forward, stuck her arm right through the dash and waved at him through the windscreen.

"Oh wow… how'd you do that?"

He touched the interior of the doors, the windows. The dash. Knocked it with a knuckle as it stayed quite solid beneath his touch.

"Takes practice. Eventually, you'll know whether by faith in God or by sheer experience that none of this is real. It's actually how I know I'm not where I should be in my faith walk. It's like a litmus test, this place."

She closed her eyes and took in a deep breath. *"I know that when I truly release every little iota of doubt it will all disappear.*

"It. Is. Finished." She repeated her personal spiritual mantra under her breath, then opened her eyes again. To his…filled with such a mixture of emotions, she couldn't even begin to interpret.

"Anyway, just know that this car is no barrier for the lost, and especially not for the fallen."

"Okay, so like I said, we need to get out of here. Right now." He looked up and around, and if his anxiety level had been palpable, she was pretty sure she'd need to hack her way through it with a machete. Or maybe a chainsaw. *"We can't just sit here in this car. What if some of the fallen show up to attack us?"*

"That's true. Once they spot us in here, for them it will be like shooting fish in a barrel."

"And you of course mean that figuratively, right?"

She considered exactly how much she should reveal to him about what the attacks she'd suffered at the hands of the fallen had entailed in the past.

"Lily?" He pulled her gaze to his with the gentle touch of his fingers beneath her chin. He searched her eyes. *"Say something, please. You're scaring the life out of me right now. Again."*

"Let's just say you'd rather not find out."

His eyes widened, then his face set into serious lines.

"Okay, so most of the ones out there are far enough away that we can probably get out before they reach us, right? Come on, the longer we delay

the worse this will get, by the looks of it, so let's get moving."

"But we don't even know what's out there," she gestured toward the open door.

"Yes, but we definitely know what's in here."

The groups were really starting to notice them now, she realized, as she saw some of them begin to nod in their direction.

"Good point. Okay, let's do this."

He pressed the instrumentation panel, and as both their doors slid up and open, he wasted no time in jumping out. Darted around to her side and extended his hand to help her climb out.

"Ready?"

She nodded, and they dashed past the dozens of curious onlookers, straight out the door.

Blinded by the sudden bright sunlight after the dimness of the room, she shaded her eyes and looked ahead. Then to the left. Somewhere in her mind, she worried that it had been a bit too easy to escape the creepy room, but some kind of transportation that actually did look like it was waiting there, especially for them, sat parked right alongside the pavement.

"See? I'll bet that right there is our way out," he pointed.

"Okay...we'll see."

They walked over to it without incident, and he grasped her hand and helped her as they both climbed into something that looked like a lovely, antique horse-drawn carriage. Open above the armrest level, on all sides, it had comfortable padded seating and even comfy looking pastel-colored blankets and throw pillows. No sooner had they settled in than they were off. They'd traveled a fair distance at quite a speed, as far as she could tell, before stopping at a crossroads. She squinted to compensate for the blurriness of everything, and the unnatural glare, and looked around.

"Maybe we should get out here. I think I saw the light that'll take us home right back there." She pointed off to left.

"Where? I don't see anything. And what light are you talking about? It's so bright out. How can you even distinguish and single out a separate light?"

"I can't explain it, but I can. There's normally a special bright light somewhere. Eventually. Most times I can sense it, even before I see it, and that tends to be the way out."

"Well, I don't see any light and look around... we're out in the middle of nowhere right now. And judging by the roadkill... Or at least what I hope and pray is actually roadkill..." He gestured to some quite unfortunate-looking organic remnants she wasn't entirely sure weren't human. *"Did you see that over there?"*

She nodded.

"We are sitting ducks right now, if some of those fallen angels you mentioned decide to approach us. I say we stay put, see where this ride goes."

"I don't know..."

She started to sense...something. But she couldn't quite figure it out.

"Well, too late now anyway. Feel that? We've started moving again."

Exactly as he said, she felt the jerk as the

carriage rolled forward and was again on the move.

She looked ahead, craned her neck to catch a glimpse of the horses. Which was no easy feat, given that for some unknown reason, the carriage looked to be at least twenty meters behind its means of propulsion. All she could see were the long leather shafts extending far out from the carriage. But there didn't seem to be any horses…

By Jove…

She'd never seen anything to compare. Distorted as her vision was, she could still see the creature pulling them along, just as it materialized out of thin air. It was super skinny and wiry, with a long hairy neck. It looked like a large and very unusual pipe cleaner, wearing a faded red and black patterned…

Was that a turban?

"Can you see that?" She pointed.

"Yeah, darndest thing I've ever seen."

"What the devil is it? It looks like a deformed dragon, suffering from malnutrition." She felt an unexpected and irrational giggle bubble up, just as the source of her amusement looked back and glared at her, with big bulging black eyes, very nearly popping out of its head. It turned back towards the road then, set its spindly little haunches down and sped up.

"Uh-oh…and I think you made him mad."

"What?! Don't be ridiculous. That thing can't understand me. Can it?"

"I'm dead serious. Did you see the look on its face right then? Seems it's not only people like us that can communicate this way. I was wondering what these were for, and now I think I know." He

grabbed a hold of the thick leather strap set into his side of the carriage near his arm. *"Better hang on because I suspect this ride is about to get really rough."*

And he wasn't wrong, as all of a sudden, they were being tossed around. Bumped up and down in their seats as the creature lifted up and reared forward. And at such a velocity, the carriage began flying right above the level of the superhighway on which they were now traveling.

Dodging cars and trucks with what she could only ascribe to alarming good fortune, it darted in and out of the heavy traffic, careening along in a completely crazy manner. It seemed to spare no thought for their safety at all in fact, as it tossed its head back, turban unraveling. The loose fabric of his head covering started blowing in the wind then, given the speed at which they were travelling. At its full length, the material stretched all the way back to them, whipping them in the face every now and then.

Afraid to let go of her grip on her side of the carriage for fear she'd tumble out; she settled for giving her head a vigorous shake. She tried to dislodge the smelly fabric, each time it struck and clung to her face and neck like a living thing.

"You know," she spat some of the stringy ends of the cloth out from between her lips as she transmitted her next thought, *"if you'd listened to me, we probably wouldn't be in this mess right now. We could have been on our way out with the light I saw."*

*"Are you kidding me? You're the one who made him mad. It's probably **because** of you we're in this mess."*

"Okay look, it does us no good to quibble about it. Just keep your eyes open for the light."

"Okay, no clue what I'm looking for, but I'll try."

"I simply can't get over how odd this all is. Granted, I've seen some pretty freaky stuff in here. It's not at all unexpected, given where we are. But this antique carriage isn't familiar to me, at all. I'm pretty certain I've never had any kind of thought or fantasy even remotely similar to this."

"That's because it's mine." He sounded sheepish.

"You've wanted to ride in a carriage?" She levelled him with an incredulous look.

"No, of course not. Not exactly..."

She doubled down on the look.

"What? When I was a kid, I had this thing for dragons, okay. There I said it. I always imagined how cool it would be to ride one."

"And this is what you pictured?"

"No," he gave a vigorous shake of his head, *"well...yes, maybe. But only partially. What can I say, I was pretty small for my age then. So maybe in my mind it was more the size of a large, scrawny lizard than a full-grown dragon?"*

"Unbelievable." She groaned and rolled her eyes as he shrugged. *"Well, guess I should be grateful we're only contending with some oddly clingy fabric, instead of staring down a fire-breather's gullet. Any clue where we're headed, Dragon-rider?"*

"Hey, you're the expert here. Your guess is probably better than mine. And ditto on the zero fire-

breathing package, by the way. That would definitely not be my idea of a good time."

"Zounds! Look out!"

Their freaky little emaciated dragon looked back and leered at her, or as close to it as she could figure. Right before, with a sudden swing to the left, they and their carriage hit the business end of a semi-truck, head-on.

She jerked awake in bed to the end of her shriek, to the echo of Jake's lingering shout, and then to the sound of her gasping breaths.

And with the eerie feeling that something quite significant was about to happen.

She's had bad experiences in the void before, and bad awakenings too, but this was different.

Because this time, it felt like dying.

Chapter 4

Proverbs 16:24
Pleasant words are as an honeycomb, sweet to the soul,
and health to the bones...

"Hey Lily, wait up!"

Jake... Fiddlesticks!

She was so hoping to make it through the day without having this conversation. She'd even left her classroom later than usual, in hopes of avoiding him. Recounting, or commiserating over their shared near-death experience of the night before, was definitely not something she either needed or desired to do that day.

In her mind, she debated whether to quicken her steps or make an all-out dash for the faculty parking lot. The option to make such a choice was removed, however, as he closed the distance between them in short order. She felt a gentle touch on the side of her right arm, took a deep breath, and turned to face him.

"I've been calling you. Didn't you get my messages?"

"Yes, I saw them."

He gestured with 'and so what?' open palms.

"And I ignored them."

"What? Why?"

"Because, I really didn't want to have to do this."

"Do what?"

"This…" she gestured with an open hand, back and forth between the two of them, "I'm not up for having the conversation you want to have right now."

"What conversation? You don't…" he turned away, then turned back, looking agitated. "Oh…dang… *I* don't even know what I want to say right now. I just–"

"You just want to know if I was actually there with you last night, right?"

He nodded.

"Well, yes. Yes, I was. But even after hearing that, your mind is still spinning. Because you're still questioning if it was as real as it felt?"

"Well, yes."

"Because if it was, then maybe you need to seek some professional help?"

Another nod.

"And you're not sure if it should be the kind of help that may very well land you in a mental institution, in a twenty-four-hour psych hold, with a Thorazine drip."

She eyed him. "Or…an exorcism."

"Seriously?"

She shrugged. "Hey, it's what you're wondering, isn't it?"

"Yes, I suppose it is." He rubbed a hand along his five o'clock shadow, and then through his hair. "How'd you know?"

"I've wrestled with those very same thoughts myself. Many, many times."

"You have? For how long? You mean these dreams, or episodes, or whatever they are, they happen often? And how many other live people like us have you seen?" He sounded alarmed as he fired off his barrage of inquiries.

"Calm down. It's been about two years, and I very rarely see others like us, and certainly not for the length of time we interacted last night. I've been trying to guess at what's causing my personal experiences."

"So, what's the verdict?"

"Well, I decided about a month after my first episode that I'm probably not crazy, and that all the evil I've encountered is somewhere out there. Not in here," she placed a hand over her chest. "So, I don't need to expel anything from myself, but what I do need is prayer, and to deepen my faith walk."

"Oh? And how's that working out for you?"

"Don't… Don't do that."

"What?"

"Don't give me that look like you think I'm wasting my time. It's a process, okay? A journey. That's why it's called a faith walk, not a faith destination. Every single time I wake up to the void, I wish I could close my eyes, say a prayer, and an Amen, and magically open them again to a normal dream, like regular people have. But it's not magic. It's supernatural and it's deeply spiritual. And things of the Spirit don't work that way. I've seen things I wouldn't even begin to know how to tell you. Personal things. Things I know way down in my soul were meant for me to learn and grow from, not only in my faith, but as a human being.

"So, am I where I'd prefer to be? Short answer is no. But in relation to where I started, and where I've been? Well, all I can say is hallelujah and praise God because I'm not where I was two years ago."

"Okay…wow. I can honestly say I was not expecting that, and I'm sorry if I sounded flippant before. I didn't mean to make light of your beliefs, in any way. I've been through my own crises of faith over the years, so believe me I know, it can take a toll. And in ways you can't ever imagine, or predict."

"Yes, I'm learning that."

"So, are you done here for the day?"

"Uh…yes. I was actually just heading home." She stepped to her left to walk past him, and he stepped with her.

"How about some dinner?"

"Uh…I have a ton of exams to grade. Maybe some other time?" She started to step to the right, and he followed her there too.

"Aww, come on Lily. You have to eat, right?"
She sighed.

"I'm not going to be able to move from this spot unless I agree to have a meal with you, am I?"

"See? I knew you were perceptive. Look at that. We're right here. Already," he waved two fingers back and forth between the arm's length distance in their gazes as his face broke into an adorable grin.

"Besides which, haven't you been charged with the Great Commission to bring in new disciples? And in that vein, shouldn't you also be helping to shepherd wayward backsliders such as myself back onto the straight and narrow?" He moved in closer.

"Really?" She looked up. Made sure precisely what she thought of his shameless pitch was quite evident in the glare she levelled on him right then.

"No. I'm dead serious. Scout's honor." He held up two fingers. "And see what I did there?" He grinned.

"Oh, for pity's sake. Of course I did." Irritated, she rolled her eyes at his reference to her given name. "But were you ever even a scout?"

"Why?"

"Because that's an old-world peace sign, you clueless lackwit."

"Okay, I'm not entirely sure what you just said, but I have an idea, and only you could insult me and make it sound *that* good. Say it again." He let out a low growl. "I think I love it when you talk dirty to me."

"Seriously?" A little girlish giggle burst out of her as his head tilted to the side with that slow smile of his.

"You are incorrigible. You know that? And by the way, the scout's sign is three closed fingers. Like this," she demonstrated.

"Oh, right… Bygones." He waved a dismissive hand.

She broke into another giggle as he gave a dry chuckle.

"So, as I was saying, can you…in all good conscience, deny *me* some much-needed spiritual counselling? After everything we went through? Together? Last night? You know I'm being quite serious when I say I could benefit from prayer, with a Holy Spirit, fire-filled, prayer warrior to get me through and over that unmitigated horror show we witnessed."

"Well, I'm no one's prayer warrior. I can tell you that right now…"

He gave her a pleading look with hands clasped together as though already in prayer.

"But…" she considered his words.

His eyes brightened.

"…I suppose…we could help each other out."

"Yes…? I'm listening…"

"I go to a Bible study at my church. There are clear reading plans with questions to meditate on and everything, but it's a pretty big group. It's quite easy to skip some of the reading sometimes and not be called out for it. So, I think I could use a reading partner. You know? So, we can encourage and hold each other accountable?"

"Say no more. I'm absolutely your guy, uh… in reading the Word, I mean. When do we start?"

"How about tomorrow? After class?" She tapped her glasses and checked her schedule. "I'm free after five. How about you?"

"Same."

"Well, okay then. We can use one of the teacher's private rooms, so we won't be disturbed. Once a week at first. Then we can see how it goes after that. We recently started reading Romans. I'll send you the lesson plan, so see how much you can get through after we get back from our evening out."

"So, you'll come to dinner?"

"Yes… I suppose I will. But…to be clear. This is not a date," she eyed him. "We're two colleagues enjoying a meal. Understood?"

"Okay, great. Whatever you say. And will do, on the scripture reading I mean. You can count on me. This is going to be amazing."

"Take it easy there, eager beaver. Let's wait and see how tomorrow goes first, before jumping to conclusions, shall we? Who's to say? You may despise the very sound of my voice in a month." She started to smile–

"Never…" His expression and crystal blue gaze reached out to her. Touched somewhere deep inside of her that she'd closed off for a very long time.

And that look effectively cancelled every glib thought, and phrase she'd considered uttering, to deny, minimize, or even outright dismiss his comment. Instead, she let it be exactly what it was.

An unexpected and very timely balm to her soul.

"So anyway," he broke their eye contact. Glanced out towards the exit doors. "I happen to know this great little Italian restaurant. It may very well be the best food in the city."

"Sure, send me the coordinates and I'll meet you there."

He smiled.

Chapter 5

Deuteronomy 30:19
I call heaven and earth to record this day against
you, that I have set before you life and death, blessing
and cursing: therefore choose life, that both thou and thy
seed may live…

Jake gave her that slow, attractive smile of his from across the table.

Strange how in the short time of their acquaintance, she'd already grown quite accustomed to basking in its warmth, but on this occasion, all she could think was, how odd?

Hadn't she already left the Italian restaurant where they'd enjoyed a very delicious dinner?

"Okay, is it just me, or did you also get a serious bout of Déjà vu right now. Feels like we did this already. Doesn't it?"

"Yes, very odd indeed…" She looked around.

"Fiddlesticks. Do you think we're in the void again? I can hear you well though. You're not in my head, I mean." She looked around again, then down at her feet to confirm what she already felt with her heels and toes. They were also the same shoes she'd put on before heading to the campus that morning. "Plus, I've got my shoes on. You?"

"Yes, me too. I–"

"So, Jake and Lily. Fancy meeting you here, and not a minute too soon."

Both she and Jake jumped and swung toward the source of the powerful voice, standing as calm as ever, with a hand resting on the back of one of the other two empty chairs at their table.

"I'm sorry, but do we know you?" Jake stood. His action putting him between her and the stranger.

She didn't know him all that well yet, but from his tone, she could tell Jake's hackles were definitely up.

"Woah, take it easy there, Jake ol' buddy. This isn't the void, and I'm only here to deliver a message. No need for all that hostility, bro. Trust me. But go to the head of the class. You got the moves for sure. See what I did there? Class? Get it? Since you're both teachers? Huh…?" He looked at them, from one to the other. "No? Really? Nothing? Wow…tough crowd." He shook his head with a smile. "Well, have no fear, that's all about to change."

She stared at him for a few moments, as did Jake she noticed. His movements slow, careful, as he reclaimed his seat beside her.

"So anyway, as I was saying, A-plus for that super strong 'defend your lady' move. And right off the bat, too. That was impressive."

"What?" She worried that her voice had elevated to the level of a shriek at his inference.

"Yeah, we'll get to that." He smiled at her. "It's like someone once said, there's always time for more questions. Am I right?" The hackle-raiser grinned with a little chuckle as Jake seemed to suddenly choke on something. He started to reach for the glass on the table in front of him, but then pulled his hand back and cleared his throat instead.

Turning to their uninvited guest again, she took in not merely his stunning smile, but also the rest of him which she could only describe later, in a saner moment, as sheer perfection.

Six-foot-six at least of sheer blond beauty, and with magnificent blue eyes that more than surpassed Jake's. And dressed to kill…in Armani?

And looking built to…well… Kill.

Massive. Powerful. Lethal. Like a German Leopard battle tank.

Only way more gorgeous.

"Mind if I sit?"

"Could we stop you?" Jake's left brow rose almost to his hairline.

"Ha! Ha! Always with the jokes this one. I like that." He turned to Jake. Slapped him on the back as he pulled the nearest chair away from the table, and given his size, sat with a masculine grace she envied. "So, let's get the obvious stuff out of the way. I'm Uriel."

"As in Archangel Uriel?" Lily wondered.

"In some circles, but I'm not one for titles. Call me Uri, please. After you've seen what I have, you'll know there can be only one title of any significance. The only one that matters and it's not mine. It's the I Am. The Alpha and Omega. The Three in One.

Amen."

"Wait… wasn't that three titles though?" Lily was confused.

"No." Uri shook his head with a smile.

"No? Really? Because I'm with Lily. I'm pretty sure that was three distinct titles."

"Oh, wait I get it. It's because for you angels when you speak, it's all one prolonged phrase, right?" she ventured.

"No. It's not about *how* we say it. It's because you don't hear… and receive its significance…in the way that we do."

She let his words marinate a minute, then…

"Wow…" she looked over at Jake and knew she likely wore the exact expression he had in that moment. "So… even the three statements…are in one… I think that was a double revelation right there. Okay…my mind is officially blown."

"You're telling me." Jake's hackles went from up to non-existent.

"Okay, so I'd say we've sufficiently broken the ice. There's more to tell, so let's take this discussion up a notch, shall we?"

"Huh?" Both she and Jake said almost at the same time.

"You'll see. Class is in session. Let's do this." Uri grinned as his hand rose in front of their faces.

SNAP!

"Zounds!" Lily put a hand up to her chest, wondering if her heart would burst out of it at any second.

"What the…? What just happened?"

Jake's head was angled downward, but not so

much she couldn't see he looked like he was about to be sick.

"It's a little rough the first time, but don't worry, you'll get accustomed to it."

"Are you saying you're planning on doing that to us again?"

"As many times as ordered."

"Is that right? Because I didn't order it the first time." Jake recovered enough to look peeved.

"True." Uri chuckled. "Only you're not the one doing the ordering, are you?"

His face took on a look of such serenity, innate wisdom, and such a transcendent glow, she wished she was a skilled enough writer to put thought to notetaker and capture it for posterity.

"Besides. Why not look around you. I'd say that momentary discomfort was all worth it, wouldn't you?"

She did as he instructed… and gaped.

They were sitting at their same table from the restaurant, only they were in the middle of a huge, breathtaking, cool, and shady oasis.

All around was lush, green, tropical foliage. Trees laden with brightly colored succulent looking fruit formed a remarkable canopy overhead through which only tiny bits of sunlight escaped to filter to the ground here and there. Creating a unique and delightful dappled pattern upon the grassy earth beneath her feet. She could hear the musical sound of water gushing out of a nearby natural water feature, and much further afield she could see the bright glare of sunshine hitting the surrounding dry and dusty desert sand.

Thinking about it, she couldn't tell if there was some invisible force keeping the desert from encroaching on their gorgeous little haven or, the other way around.

"It looks like Shakespeare's *The Tempest* meets the Sahara," she whispered in wonder.

"Exactly… Lily. Jake. Welcome to your D.I.E.T. Well, technically this is yours Lily, so hope you don't mind sharing."

"I'm sorry?" She thought she'd misheard.

Did he just say–?

"Not diet as in meal plan. It's an acronym for your Dream Implementation, Elevation, and Transformation experience. It's our way of counteracting the negative impacts of the void. Plus, you might learn a thing or two, along the way. If you're open to it. Look around you now. What do you see?"

"A whole lot of greenery," Jake stated the obvious.

"Yes, but it's the contrast that gets me." Lily looked out at the desert and then back in at the beauty in which they were sitting. "It's the ultimate choice, isn't it? Death and emptiness, versus life. Bleak separation and desolation…or Paradise."

"Okay, now that's deep…" Jake looked like he'd received another timely revelation.

"Similar to life's choices, some can leave you empty and wanting, while others fill you up. It really depends on your perspective, and what you're willing to grab a hold of… as you simultaneously let go." Uri smiled.

"That's so interesting…" Lily pondered his

words.

"So, I guess the next question is, why us?"

"I'm glad you asked, Jake. Your nation and indeed the world is heading into a perilous time in your history. Earth's resident aliens, Verndari, as they call themselves, are not what they appear to be. But you both already know that, right? You may not have guessed what they are. Or figured out how or why, but somewhere deep inside you've always known."

"Like Neo, in *The Matrix*," Jake suggested.

"Right?" She touched Jake on the arm. "That's exactly what I was thinking. You've seen it?"

"I think everyone's seen it." Uri nodded. "What is it with you and watching all those old movies? Don't you have anything else to do in this century? If I didn't know better, I'd think you're all characters in a book series written by someone living in the last century, who's got no other frame of reference."

They all had a chuckle at that.

"So, at the risk of learning some other freaky bit of info I'd rather not know, who are the defenders, exactly?"

"The fallen. The one third of angels who fell from home eons ago. We, my brothers and I, the true servants of our God, call them exiles."

"How very apt. I like that." She nodded.

"That... That's your takeaway after hearing we've all been going to hell in a moon transport for the last thirty-five years since Verndari arrived?" Jake's look spoke volumes.

"What? It fits. Also, you have to admit, it's quite clever."

"Plus," Uri added, "they've been right here with you a whole lot longer than thirty-five years. You just couldn't see them."

"Definitely not what I needed to hear right then." She suppressed a little shiver as she felt her pores raise.

Jake turned back to Uri.

"So, what do we do? What does it all mean, in real terms?"

"It means you have a unique opportunity to do your part to push back the forces of evil at this very moment in earth's history. All over the globe, the human resistance is growing, as more and more people, like you, are waking up…to their dreams. Literally.

"The exiles are growing restless. They know their time is short, as they seek to deceive and steal away as many souls as they can from the love of our God. Make no mistake, their moment of reckoning has long since come and gone. They have been judged and punished. In every dimension. They are done. In this world and the next. They're banking and still existing on the fact that far too many of you…simply don't know, or believe it…yet."

"Wow…you mean we're doing this to ourselves? Keep on inviting evil in day after day? Well, that's a scary statement, if I ever heard one." Lily let his words sink in and play havoc with her soul.

"You're telling me. Now that was a revelation on steroids." Jake looked pensive.

"So, as a result, you will notice their attacks are becoming more brazen and erratic, and in their haste, they have become careless. Their dream infiltration is increasingly clumsy and more clunky. Instead of vague recollections of odd sights and feelings, people are having full-on experiences they can only describe in their limited awareness as alien abduction. As their living souls are ripped out of their sleeping bodies.

"No more nighttime offerings of veiled inducements for joining with evil. No. Rather, they've largely resorted to torturing and tormenting believers, in some ludicrous attempt to make them think their faith is misplaced, or ineffectual because of the presence of such evil in their nocturnal subconscious.

"Instead, it has had the complete opposite effect. Propelling God's faithful to seek His presence, His infinite wisdom, grace, mercy, and protection in ever greater numbers. In the Underground movement, in homes, churches, places of business and learning, people are trading stories of the sustaining, saving power of the Almighty in the face of unspeakable and vile terror. And because of that very fact, the face of evil grows even more rage-filled, and more spiteful, in a never-ending malicious cycle of unparalleled chaos."

"Okay, so is it weird the first thought in my head right now is thank God, I'm not crazy?" Jake put a hand up to his head.

"So, now who's got the inappropriate takeaway?" Lily tapped Jake's hand. "But yes, I must admit, the thought did cross my mind too."

"Wait...no offence Uri, but how do we know this isn't just another elaborate deception? Another freaky trip to the void?" Jake ventured.

"No," she said before the angel could respond. "This feels different. I've never seen such beauty sustained for this long, and with this much depth and clarity." She looked around again at their heaven-inspired garden vista.

"Here, try one of these." Uri pointed to a large, woven tray resting on the table in front of them that was overladen with fruit of every kind, and in vivid hues. A tray she was pretty sure wasn't there until he pointed to it.

"Woah. That's amazing. Did you see that?" Jake's eyes widened.

She nodded, as they both reached out and selected a piece of the fruit on offer.

"Okay, so this is the sweetest, most luscious strawberry I've ever tasted in my entire life." She grabbed another off the tray and ate that one too. "Okay, I was wrong, this one is." She selected two more.

"It's really good, right?" Uri grinned in obvious appreciation of the pleasure they were deriving from consuming some of the bounty in front of them.

"You know, I think it's getting better and better every time I take a bite," Jake spoke around another big mouthful of the peach he was eating. "How is that even possible?" He sucked up some of the juice that ran down to his wrist.

"Well Uri, you've convinced me," she licked her own fingertips, "there's absolutely no way we're in the void right now. Everything I've ever tried to eat in there tasted nothing like it should. Usually watered down and dull, and with the consistency of paste. The fallen could never replicate or recreate the amazing good things of God, not even if their lives depended on it. This is most definitely not them. In fact, if this isn't my first little taste of heaven, I don't know what is."

"Not even close, but I'm glad you're enjoying it all the same."

"Enjoying it? Are you kidding me? Enjoyment doesn't even begin to describe the sensations I'm experiencing right now. We need to come up with a new word for this. I'm feeling my own pleasure magnified, alongside the fruit's joy at being consumed. I can't even explain it. This is crazy! Lily? Do you feel it too?"

She nodded. "Oh yes. Ethereal is as close as I can come to describing it. After this, I may never be able to stomach eating in the real world again."

"Don't worry, you will." Uri assured her. "What you're feeling is unique to the D.I.E.T. You'll remember it was great, but there'll be no way for you to compare, so you'll derive just as much enjoyment as you normally do from the foods you ordinarily consume."

"I'd like to say good to know, but it's actually not." She shook her head on a quirky smile. "Know what I mean?"

"Oh, it's a quandary to be sure." Jake returned her smile. "An impossible choice where you don't know what's more of a loss, not being able to have this in the real world, or, not being able to recognize why you should miss having this in the real world."

"Exactly!" She polished off another delectable, plump, and juicy strawberry. "Oh, bless God, I see what you mean, Jake. I swear I can sense the piece of fruit is grateful for me eating and enjoying it," she said around her mouthful. "This…is amazing."

She turned back to Uri.

"Did I imagine that?"

"No, the sensations are as real as you are."

He smiled and she imagined the brightness of his face could probably be seen from miles away. He was the Archangel of Illumination, right? Not only in terms of philosophical enlightenment, but also in the way he physically reflected God's light? It certainly was a fitting title.

"How is this even possible?"

"Because it's exactly where it's meant to be, and doing precisely what it was created to do – to bring nourishment and joy with unending gratitude."

"I know I said it before…but wow."

"Ditto," Jake registered his agreement with an enthusiastic and sticky thumbs up.

"So, you haven't said yet, what do you need us to do in a practical sense?"

"Only what you're trained and blessed to do. Lead your flock. You don't need to reveal to your students what they really are, but you can at every possible opportunity show them Verndari are not who they pretend to be. They are fake saviors. The fact they chose to call themselves defenders is an affront to humanity of the highest order. You both have an ideal platform and a captive audience. So, start using it to your best advantage. The other universities and colleges will soon follow. In the vein of the Anti-War Movement and the Civil Rights Movement of the nineteen-sixties, and again in the late twenty-twenties, you need only agitate for meaningful change and sit back and watch the righteous rebellion sprout and grow amongst the younger generation. They are the ones poised to make a real difference in this fight. And don't be afraid to engage them with references to your faith. You'll be surprised at just how many of them will be receptive to it."

"You know, this is probably perfect timing. I've been thinking a lot about us holding a couple rallies to raise awareness about the dangers of the chip tech the defenders have been implanting in so many of the less fortunate these days. That branding they're doing is nothing short of barbaric. I hear they're even actively targeting college-aged students with all sorts of inducements on social media. It would be quite a slap in the face for them if those very same kids turned out to be at the forefront of the movement speaking out against it. I was going to introduce the idea of an organized protest to my philosophy students first and then the pol sci group after that."

"That's a great idea," she nodded. "I know my lot would be fully into that idea, too. They absolutely adore a righteous cause. What do you think of that Uri?"

"I think that's as good a place to start as any."

"Okay, so we have a plan. Lily? Let's meet, later today? We can start to work out the logistics. Oh, and I've got a good friend who works with the NYPD. Yes, I'm sure Duncan can help us get the demonstration permits arranged, if we need them… Lily?"

"Huh?" She looked up. "Sorry, what'd you say?

Not sure I caught that last bit." She continued petting a tiny creature that had wandered over as they were speaking.

"Okay, now what in the name of all that's holy is that?"

"In truth, I don't really know. A fairy or sprite's pet, maybe? No clue. Something from *A Midsummer Night's Dream?* Only, way cuter. Aren't you? Yes, you are. Cute as a button. And definitely much cuter than a certain mangy, freaky little dragon-lizard we know." She felt her heart melt as it looked up at her with doe eyes and leaned into her leg as she brushed its cuddly little body covered in soft blue fur.

"Unbelievable..."

Jake shook his head, while Uri grinned.

Chapter 6

Proverbs 31:8-9
Open thy mouth for the dumb in the cause of all such as
are appointed to destruction. Open thy mouth, judge
righteously, and plead the cause of the poor and needy...

"Okay. So, can anyone tell me what this is?"

Jake looked out across his new group, saw a couple familiar faces from his Pol-Sci classes. But even the ones he recognized joined in with the sea of blank looks, and just as many shrugs that he was receiving at that moment.

"Really? No one? Okay, well then tell me how it makes you feel when you look at it. What emotions does it elicit?"

"Sadness? I think he looks totally depressed," one young woman ventured.

"No, I think he looks pensive," another person offered.

"No offence, Professor, but I think that guy looks like he's about to take a serious... I mean an epic dump."

At which time the entire class broke into laughter.

"No… Travis. Really? Not even close, and bordering on irreverent as always, I see." He shook his head on a dry chuckle as the laughter died down. "Well, if Trav's perspective is any indication of where this is headed, allow me to end the suspense with one more question. What was the common denominator in what each of those three people had to say?"

Another shrug-fest ensued.

"They all expressed their particular perspective by starting with the phrase 'I think.' And that state of being is exactly what this depicts."

He pointed to the life-sized 3-D representation that was making a slow spin in a circle as it made its journey all around the classroom, right above the heads of his students.

"What you're looking at, ladies and gentlemen, is a bronze sculpture aptly called 'The Thinker'. It was crafted a long time ago, around 1904, by the renowned artist Auguste Rodin. And as you can see, it portrays a nude male, seated atop a large rock. And no… still not a toilet Trav," he paused for another short round of laughter, "and he's in a contemplative pose. Rodin himself made more than ten castings of the original, and after his death, the French government obtained the rights to make many more than that. They can be seen all around the globe in the world's best museums now.

"This is likely the quintessential, iconic image of all that the study of philosophy embodies. It's about introspection and contemplation. Deep thought and reflection. So, all that to say, that in this class over the next semester and beyond, we'll be covering all the main elements of philosophy this sculpture is intended to bring to your minds. It's origins and history. Principles and also viewpoints from the past.

"Now some of the basic topics you may already be familiar with, which is great. For example, logic. We'll explore and learn about sound methods for distinguishing good from bad reasoning. Or ethics and morality, where we'll examine values of right and wrong, good and bad, justice and injustice, with some very practical and topical examples.

"For instance, right off the top of your head, what do you think about the chip implantation centers Verndari have instituted for the less fortunate who want to access their food banks now?"

Silence.

"Come on, anyone? This is a safe space. You can feel free to discuss anything and everything here, without fear of repercussions."

A small group off to the right looked from one to another and then a hesitant hand went up from among them.

"Yes," he looked down at the session electronic seating chart, "Gwenyth. What a lovely name."

"Thank you, Professor." He saw the anxiety in her face relax a bit. "So...I, well we, a group of us...we were thinking that it's immoral, and dangerous. And that it shouldn't have been allowed to happen."

"Thank you, for your candor. You are absolutely to be commended for speaking out. It's difficult and frightening to do that in the shadow of such a formidable force as the defenders present themselves, isn't it?"

She nodded.

"I believe we're fast approaching a time on earth when men and women will look back and point to this time as a watershed moment in our history. A time when we'll collectively wonder if we did enough, and said enough to safeguard our way of life, our freedom, our humanity, even our very existence. In the face of creeping tyranny.

"You know, there's a famous line that was at one stage attributed to an eighteenth-century Irish statesman and philosopher named Edmund Burke, and I quote, 'the only thing necessary for evil to triumph, is for good men to do nothing.' It was eventually proven that he didn't actually say it, but regardless of how it originated, I think we can all agree it's a powerful statement. Yes?"

Several individuals nodded and sounded their agreement.

"So, can it be scary and intimidating to voice an opinion that's perceived to be unpopular? Absolutely. But it is in these times that we absolutely must. And in the fine tradition of institutions of learning all over the globe this is just the place to do it. The mechanism and the medium to best advance any and every righteous cause. To make your voices heard alongside those of kindred mind. And who knows? You may well find your opinion isn't quite as unpopular as you thought, and it's in fact shared by a whole lot more people than you imagined.

"I see some of you looking skeptical. Maybe you don't think it's a cause you want to get involved with, or support," he shrugged, "because you know where your next meal is coming from, you don't need what the defenders are offering. Well, what I'll say to you is if you think it's a "them" and not a "me" situation, think again. Whatever wealth you have today could be gone tomorrow. An economic downturn could plunge this country into a severe depression in a matter of months. Or it could be another global pandemic, like the first and the worst. Thank God we've put multiple safeguards in place since then. But you've all heard, or read about it. The one that crashed economies and killed millions of people in 2020? God forbid, but it could be a death, or serious illness in your families. Your financial status could change for any number of reasons.

"So, all of that to say, don't delude yourself. Because there are none deserving. And there are none good. There are only men, and women, and children who could die, when those who could make a difference stay silent. Remember that.

"I, and a couple of other teachers, have been getting ready to hold some rallies around campus to raise awareness about this and other issues surrounding the defender agenda. Anyone interested in helping to organize support, or who maybe wants to attend to find out some more about the real dangers we're facing as a nation and in the world, please, stay back and talk with me after class.

"Okay, so that was my political speech for today. Oh wait, wrong class."

A round of chuckles and laughter rose up at his comment.

"Right, where were we–" he consulted his notetaker, "–oh, right. I also want to introduce you to some topics in philosophy you maybe haven't heard about before today. Now, here's where it gets really interesting. I'm talking Metaphysics, which investigates the nature of reality, existence, identity, time, space, causality, and the relationship between mind and matter. Or Epistemology, which is merely a fancy term for the study of knowledge, belief, and justification.

"I know it's a whole lot to take in right away, but don't worry because essentially, we'll be discussing ideas. Right and wrong, good and bad. We'll explore the entire spectrum of thought and hopefully at the end of it, and if I do my job right," he smiled, "you'll actually learn something. So, what do you say we get started?"

Chapter 7

Psalms 38:4
For mine iniquities are gone over mine head: as an
heavy burden they are too heavy for me…

"**Come on, Dad,** where are you? We already started down without you."

"Okay, keep your boots on. I'm coming." Jake rounded the sharp curve in time to see Sam expertly repel off the steep side of the cliff face they'd just scaled nearly to the summit, and were now descending to return to base camp.

"Attagirl!" He cupped a hand to his mouth and called down as he looked over the edge to follow her progress as she navigated her way along the exposed strata.

"Well, you certainly took your time, Professor."

He turned at the sound of Lily's cultured, pleasantly mellifluous voice, and very nearly lost his breath, for the hundredth time that day.

"Hey, all part of the plan. Did you miss me?" He winked at her and then grinned as she rolled her eyes.

"Thanks again for doing this, Lil. I know you only planned on dinner tonight with Sam and me. Not scaling a cliff with most of our hiking club, for half the day." He grinned. "I'm so glad you agreed to come climbing with us. I truly want Sam to feel she has a strong female role model she can rely on whenever she doesn't want to confide in dear old dad. Know what I mean? And this is such a great way for you two to get to know each other."

"Oh, don't even worry about it. I am thoroughly enjoying this." She shaded her eyes as she took a look over the side. "Sam's wonderful. You should be so proud of her."

"Oh, I am."

"Plus, look at her go. She's great at this, isn't she?"

She grasped the safety line and bent over as she gazed down at Sam.

"Yeah, she's something all right…" he agreed.

And so are you…

The words were right there, on the tip of his tongue and in the forefront of his mind, but he held them back, knowing it was way too soon for talk like that. He tried to think of something else to say to distract himself.

Anything else.

But it was nearly impossible, when standing before him was a Lily he'd never even imagined, in his wildest fantasies. When all he could think was that her beauty, her grace and poise. In fact, everything about her was quite simply…breathtaking.

Dressed in a cute little figure-hugging tank top, and sweatpants that showed off her eye-catching curves and shapely legs to perfection. Soft, brown skin glowing in the sunlight, his mocha goddess come to life was nothing short of stunning. Everything he could have ever hoped for, and so much more.

Her hair, almost always confined to a nine-to-five, yet still ever so slightly disheveled, sexy-cute bun, was now loose. Falling well beyond her shoulders in all its thick, deep brown, and free for the weekend glory.

He gave her his smile as she glanced over at him. She lifted a hand, brushed away a few long wavy strands that fell across her cheek and inviting lips. Those very lips he longed to kiss, parted, as her lovely face lit with her return smile. All while her soulful brown eyes, with their exotic little tilt at the corners, thanks to her mixed ancestry, beckoned to him as sure as a siren song to a mariner of old. And just like that, he let his gaze wander where it would.

"I'll bet it's all thanks to you, huh?"

"Sorry? How do you mean?"

He'd been so caught up in his gawk-fest, he completely forgot what she was talking about right then.

Make meaningful eye contact, and listen to what she's saying, man...

He pulled his gaze away from her butt and zeroed in on her eyes and what she was saying.

"I only meant I'm sure you're the number one reason Sam's such a skilled mountaineer. Aren't you? I bet you're a champion rock climber." She slid over to him and he very nearly lost it as he caught a tantalizing whiff of her hair. Vanilla…and something delicious, and fruity. His favorite combination…

Stifling a primal growl, he forced himself to focus on what she was saying once more.

"Yes. You strike me as a man of a certain…prowess." She gazed up at him. Ran a slow finger up his arm from his wrist to his bare shoulder. Funny, he didn't feel it half as much as he imagined he would, now she'd finally touched him in a way he'd only ever dreamed of before…

"Wha–?" He started to ask, but then called out in fear instead as, without warning, she bumped him, shoving him right off the side of the mountain.

He felt a suffocating knot of fear and anxiety choke any sound he might have made, when just as quickly, she caught him by his right hand. He looked up, even as he scrambled for a toehold. Found he couldn't move his other arm as it was restrained behind him…somehow.

But it was no longer Lily looking down at him. It was Gwen.

The atmosphere turned cold, as the area around him on the mountainside and in the surrounding sky grew dark and ominous.

"Imagine bumping…into you, way out here, Jake. Wait, was that insensitive? My bad. Look at you. Hanging on for dear life. And just like me…absolutely no one is coming to save you… What? No words of wisdom for this situation, Professor? Like you had for your students in your class today? Oh well, guess you deserve this then." She smirked at him then let go.

Feeling that his heart would explode in his chest as he fell backwards, something suddenly bumped him out of midair, and right into the side of the cliff face.

He jerked awake with a shout.

Unable to control the shaking in his limbs, he felt the damp cling of his bed sheets at his waist. Every inch of him was covered in a drenching cold sweat. He put a hand to his bare chest for a moment, where his heart was pounding out a rapid rhythm.

He rotated his right arm slowly in its socket as he sat up. Winced at the very real and lingering throb in his shoulder from being suspended and then slammed into the nightmare-inspired jagged rock face.

And with the also very real sensation of deep dread resting like a brick in the pit of his stomach.

A feeling such as he'd never known.

And even worse than the day he'd killed his ex-wife.

Chapter 8

Romans 14:12
So, then every one of us shall give account of
himself to God...

"Hey, Trudy. How are you?" Lily greeted her newest friend. "So glad I bumped into you out here. Didn't you say you knew someone who does English lessons on the side? One of my students really needs some help with his grammar. I'd do it myself, but I simply don't have the time."

"Oh yes, sure. Just give me his deets and I'll see what I can do to help. Speaking of which…that situation over there, that can't be good, right?"

Gertrude Susan Robinson pursed her lips and shook her head, as her chin tipped up a bit to their left. The university's brilliant and quirky professor of chemical engineering, she was a self-professed nerd and often joked about the aptness of the acronym for her name – G.S.R., being the same as the one for gunshot residue. Particularly since she'd spent a large portion of her early career analysing a fair amount of it during her stint in the NYPD's forensics department.

"I'm thinking your boy over there looks like *he* could use some serious help, right about now."

Lily looked over and saw Jake standing with a young woman some distance away. She was speaking in an animated fashion, and every now and again she reached out to touch him, while he shifted from foot to foot.

"Who's that with him?"

"That my friend is Jeri Baldwell. She transferred in around the same time you did. I met her at the last full faculty staff meeting."

"Really? Wow. Looking like that… I thought maybe she was a student. She's dressed like a…uh…a–"

"Like a straight-up hooker? Go on, you can say it."

She gasped.

"Come on now. Don't pretend you weren't thinking it. Uh-huh." She grinned as a giggle burst from Lily.

"And she's teaching Sex Ed over on the eighth quad, if you can believe that. Talk about her life imitating her career."

"Wow. For real?"

"Oh, I kid you not. How I long for the days when Sex Ed used to be about teaching safe practices, ONLY when all encouragement towards abstinence failed. Now it's practically a how-to-porno."

"Yes, so I've heard. I suppose it's chock-a-block?"

"Oh, yeah. If that quirky expression of yours means young men from the floor right up to the 3-D light installations. Quite a few girls too, but less than the boys obviously. You didn't hear this from me but I'm told she's the genuine article. Used to be an adult film star and everything. Well, before she got her degree to teach."

"Guess she figured she'd gathered enough experience to share?"

"Guess so. What is she even doing here at this time of the day, anyway? I happen to know her next class should have started five minutes ago."

"How would you know that?"

"Because I'm friends with the guy who teaches the religious studies sessions at this same time, right next door. He says he always has to get into his class early, to avoid getting trampled by the stampede into hers. I mean, talk about poor scheduling. Religious studies? Right next door to 'Daisy does Dallas', I mean seriously?"

"Oh wow." Lily suppressed a sharp giggle at Trudy's obscure reference to a joke involving the adult film industry.

"Yes, and then some. Good thing the rooms are soundproof. Whoever did the room roster for this semester should be fired. Anyway, as I said, it's pretty much standing room only. I hear they had to turn at least a dozen students away last semester. And that was when an old guy with bad hygiene was teaching the class. I forget his name. Can't even imagine what it'll be like now with Ms. Everything-you-wanna-know-about-sex-in-a-too-tight-skirt over there."

"I suppose that look appeals to some?"

Trudy looked over at Jake. Her chin tilted up for a second.

"Hmm… But not him though. He looks like he wants out."

"You think so?"

"Are you kidding me? Just look at him. I haven't seen anyone that uncomfortable since I reminded my husband about his yearly prostate exam." She barked out a laugh. "I'm telling you that man needs saving. So, what are you waiting for? An embossed invitation? Go on. Go over there and help him out." Trudy pushed her a bit in their general direction.

"Me? Why me? Why don't you do it?"

"Because I'm a mostly happily married woman and everyone knows it. Look at him. He needs someone to claim ownership." Her brows raised as she gave a firm nod and smiled. "Trust me."

"Claim ownership? What? Me? No-ooo. How would I even–"

"Go over there, plant one on him and call him your baby daddy, that'll scare her off for sure." She let out a wicked little cackle.

"What?! I will do no such thing. Absolutely not."

"Oh, lighten up. I'm only kidding. Go, stare up into those gorgeous, dreamy blue eyes and call him your favourite distraction, or your King. Everyone knows men love that kind of talk from their lady, so she'll be guaranteed to get the message from the jump that he's off limits."

"And after that?"

"He's a friend of yours, isn't he? Just use that. Go on. Git! You'll think of something else to say, I'm sure. By the time you get over there."

"Well, he did ask me to meet him earlier.   We both have a break right now. That's why I was out here. So…I suppose I could–"

"See? There you go." Her new friend's shove this time was none too gentle and had her quickening her step to avoid an embarrassing stumble. She glanced back and saw Trudy shoo her with flicking hands as she mouthed the words, "Go on. You can do it."

"There you are…uh, Jake! Darling!" She called out as she approached the pair. "I've been looking for you everywhere since your Philosophy 101 ended." She reached between them, grasped his forearm and dropped her voice to a low and sexy rumble. "Well, aren't you looking like my very favourite guilty pleasure today." She raked him with a bold gaze she knew Jeri couldn't miss.

Reaching up, she gave him a pointed look right in the eyes in return for his super shocked one. Then pulled on his arm to get him to lean down so she could place a warm kiss on his reddening cheek.

"Who's this?" She feigned ignorance and turned towards Jeri without relinquishing her hold on his arm. Even caressed it for good measure. Sure. That's how his girlfriend would act. Right?

"Oh…uh," he cleared his throat, "Lil, meet Jeri. Jeri…Lily is…uh…"

"I'm Lily Kavanagh," she extended her hand, "Jake's girlfriend. So nice to meet you, Jeri, was it?

Can't recall seeing you in this quad before. I'm an English lit professor here. And you are?"

"Oh, well I'm fairly new here too, so that's prob'ly why you haven't seen me before. I'm into sex ed." She licked her lips as she delivered that bit of information as though she was referencing a recreational preference, rather than her chosen curriculum. And in Jake's general direction at that.

Seriously?

Funny how she managed to make it sound absolutely nothing like a course taught on campus, the way she said it.

"Really? Is that right? Well, isn't that…uh…curious?" She looked up at Jake and opened her eyes super wide. He grinned.

She turned back to Jeri, "Well, good for you."

"Oh yeah. My students love my classes. They're eating them up. How about you? How are yours enjoying…what was is it you said? English?"

"Literature. Yes. I'd have to say so far so good. They seem to be taking to the classics in particular, like ducks to water."

"Yeah, just like you, I'm sure." She smiled at her in a way that only another woman would interpret and understand as the drawing of relationship rivalry combat lines.

Plus… Wait… Was that some sort of thinly veiled crack about age?

Did she just call me old? Really? Oh, no… She did not disrespect me like that. What-Ho! The games afoot and the battle of wits hath most decidedly commenced in earnest.

"Why, thank you. That's quite a compliment." She graced her with a confident half smile.

"Oh? How do you figure that?"

"Well, the older literary works are all renowned for being incredibly difficult to acquire. I happen to have quite a collection of them. Take Shakespeare and Hemingway for instance. They're subtle, literary masterpieces of unquestionable and intrinsic quality. Always of far higher value, and much more sought after, and treasured, than the newer, in-your-face, modern rubbish that's a dime a dozen…and oh, *so easy* to get, right now."

Her smile was demure.

As Jeri glared at her.

And as Jake turned his sudden bark of laughter into a fake cough. Or two.

"Are you all right, sweetheart?" She took a moment to pat, then rub his back.

"Uh, yes. I'm fine. Must be my allergies, probably." He hid a grin behind his hand, as he coughed again.

"Well," Jeri huffed and glared at her again, "uh…I've always thought that actually doing…uh…stuff, trumps reading about it. Every time."

"Oh, really? And I've always thought that the people who think that way are merely attempting to compensate for the fact that they lack even an iota of the imagination that would allow them to truly appreciate the finer more elusive things in life. Like a priceless piece of art, and yes, a classic novel. Go figure. Perhaps we're both wrong."

Jeri's mouth opened then closed again, as though she'd made the wise choice to quit while she was behind.

But then again…

"Yes, well anyway, Jake, as I was saying, I sure hope you and I will get to cross paths like this again. Prob'ly, super often from now on…considering…" she flashed him a sultry smile as she ignored Lily and turned her gaze on him.

*Considering? Considering **what** exactly? Oh, no…this brazen daughter of a guttersnipe hussy did not just disrespect me like that. AGAIN!*

It was as if she didn't even see her. Standing right there.

"Hmm," she crossed her arms then tapped a fingernail to her chin, "that's unlikely, isn't it, though? What with your classes in…what was it again? Constitutional Law?"

"Sex Ed," Jeri bit out.

"Right, right. My bad. So, correct me if I'm wrong, but aren't those classes all held in the eighth quad?"

"Uh, yeah. So?"

"So, I'd say that's quite a distance to travel given we…Jake and I that is, are all the way out here in the first. Take today for instance. I'll bet you had to duck out right before your next class started and what? Take a hover-cab to get all the way over here like this? Not a good look. Just reeks of desperation, don't you think?"

Jeri's mouth opened then closed again, like a fish out of water. Soundless and bewildered.

"All-righty then. That's what I figured."

She turned to Jake. Popped her chin up, gave him a sultry half smile, and dropped her tone an octave "Hey, Trouble…"

"Uh-huh…"

To his credit, he played it to the hilt. Gave her that look…like a man consumed. All steamy intriguing intent…and bad-boy testosterone.

And she revelled in it.

"I'd say it's time to go. We've got that *thing*, remember?"

He nodded once. His answering smile probably rivalling her own on the heat scale. "Oh, right babe, definitely. Wouldn't want us to be late for the, uh…thing." He grasped one of her hands between both of his. "We should go. Now."

"You'll have to excuse us, Jeri. So glad we had this opportunity to chat though. Always so lovely to hear about what's happening with the psych majors."

"Sex Ed!" Jeri's shout was so strident Lily imagined it echoed off the nearest quad wall.

"Isn't that what I said?" She feigned ignorance. "Well, anyway, you take good care now," she waved a casual hand as she let Jake lead her away.

He placed the hand he held into the crook of his elbow, leaned down, and whispered near her ear, "Wow. Thank you for saving me. She's been after me since we met at the last faculty meeting." He glanced back over his shoulder. "Seems she's still standing there. Watching us leave."

"Probably still in shock." She giggled.

"Most likely." He grinned. "You are amazing, by the way. That was quite a performance. I think I just became your biggest fan."

"I must confess, I rather enjoyed that. You're looking at the woman voted best drama student in my university club two years running. We're talking class of eighteen, AND nineteen." She felt a strut coming on and shamelessly gave in to it.

"Well, okay then. Remind me never to cross you, Professor. That was formidable." He held out a fist.

"You better know it," she bumped it with her own, then snapped her hand wide open. "Oorah!"

"Well, that was probably more of a 'boo yah' moment, but I'll take it." He gave her a quirky smile. "So, class of nineteen, huh?" He glanced at her off and on, as they strolled along arm-in-arm in the sunshine. "That would make you what? Thirty-four, thirty-five?"

"Thirty-eight, actually. Thought you didn't venture over the prickly precipice of discussing ladies' ages?"

"Hey, you put it out there. I'm only doing the math." He grinned.

"Uh-huh… with a casual mention of only two of the years I spent in university? Practically needed an actuary to work that one out, didn't you? But by all means," she pulled her hand free to make air quotes with her fingers, "I, 'put it out there,' after all." She grinned back.

He barked out a laugh, "Okay, okay…you got me." He glanced back over his shoulder again, grasped her hand, and resettled it in the crook of his arm.

"And what about you?"

She tugged on the forearm she was holding. "How old are you, Professor?"

"Forty-six and proud of it."

"Well, good for you. You know, you don't look a day over fifty-five."

"Really?" He eyed her.

"Oh, come on. I'm kidding, of course." She giggled. "Fine specimen of a man such as yourself. I actually thought you were only in your early forties when we met at the store. You look *so* good." She pulled back a bit. Let her gaze take a slow trip over his very attractive frame, with blatant appreciation.

He dismissed her compliment with a wave of a hand, but she could tell he was pleased.

"Well, I'm healthy, bless God. That's all I care about. I needed to stay fit to keep up with Sam. Taking care of a kid on your own is no joke."

"I can well imagine."

"When she was a toddler, I remember thinking how crazy it was that someone so small could run that fast. She'd tear around the house like a whirlwind, and there I was, trying to catch up. Calling out, "Where yuh going? Where yuh going?" I'd run after her, terrified she'd break everything in sight." He shook his head with a chuckle as she smiled.

"That must have been quite an experience. If you don't mind me asking, how old was she, when you and your ex, split?"

"Not at all. She'd just turned thirteen."

"Oh, wow…that must have been so tough."

"You have no idea. That was when I started longing for the days when my biggest problem was chasing after her so she wouldn't break stuff. That was heaven, compared to what I faced raising a teenaged girl on my own.”

“So, your wife didn’t help raise your daughter at all?”

“No, my *ex*-wife…she, uh…she left us.”

“Oh, my gosh. I’m so sorry. In the store when you spoke about your relationship with your daughter…I just assumed–”

“You assumed I was the one out of the family picture. It’s okay. It’s what most people think. But no. I’m the one who raised Sam alone, from thirteen. But for the grace of God, they say.”

“Oh, that’s so true. I don’t envy you. I remember what I was like at that age.”

“You know, we should have dinner sometime. The three of us.”

“Oh, yes. Sure. I’d love that.”

“Well… maybe not, after you hear why I’m offering.”

“Oh no, don’t tell me…more Garrett trouble?”

“Oh no, he’s history. She’s onto another one now. Now it’s Dauntless trouble, if you can believe that.”

“Excuse me?”

“Yes, you heard me right. Apparently, his parents were big fans of those 21st century *Divergent* books and movies.”

“Wow…and here I thought *I* had issues with the name lottery.”

“Right? Little did you know. You could have had the dubious honour of being dubbed Amity… or…or, Candor, or–”

"Erudite!" They both said at the same time and laughed.

"Oh, that's so funny."

"What's funny is the kid is anything but fearless. Looks like he's about to throw up every time she's brought him over to the house."

"What'd you do? Bring your laser repeater to the door?" She grinned.

"Are you being serious right now?"

"What? You strike me as someone who'd be quite intimidating in a meet the parent type situation."

"You know, I can't decide what's more worrying. The fact you think I'm *that* kind of dad, or, that I own a dangerous firearm like you said."

"Is there any other kind?"

She shrugged as he looked incredulous.

"Oh, relax. I'm only having a bit of fun." She chuckled.

"Well, I'll have you know I'm usually the very picture of chill when she brings over a boyfriend."

"You?! You have got to be joking." She barked out a laugh. "You, Jake Traynor, are anything but chill. Every time you set those blue peepers on me the words that come to mind are intense and laser focused…and fierce. Oh, and perhaps with a soupçon of maniac thrown in for good measure."

He burst out laughing as she grinned.

"Me? A maniac? Oh, come on now, Lil. What about me says crazy?"

"I don't know. It's something in the eyes." She stopped walking and he did too. Heard her own breathing in the stillness of the day as she stared up at him. "Sometimes you look at me and… I don't know… I feel like there's something lurking there. Something I've never seen before. In anyone. I can't describe it, but I just know it makes me feel…"

"Feel what…?" His voice was soft as he gazed down at her.

"A bit odd…and ever so slightly…nervous..."

…Of myself…

Is what she wanted to say. But didn't. Because the truth was, he was making her feel things she didn't want to acknowledge. Things she hadn't felt in over a year.

Or maybe never.

Hearing the beep of her fifteen minutes to session reminder, she broke their eye contact and glanced back over her shoulder. "So, is she still looking? I've got to get back to class."

"Oh… no, she left already." He cleared his throat, but his voice still sounded deep, with a tempting hint of gravel. "I only wanted to walk with you like this for a while longer."

"Really? I don't believe you." Smiling, she slapped at his arm and started to pull away as he chuckled.

"That's actually why I called you to meet me. It's such a beautiful day out. I thought you'd enjoy taking a break with me, out on the benches, or for a stroll in the sunshine. So, thank you, my lady. A pleasure as always." He caught her hand before she could escape and bent at the waist as he lifted it to his mouth.

He drew her gaze to his…as he tilted his head to the side. Gave her the very same intense, heated look she'd described a scant minute before, and then doubled the ante, as she watched him press a soft but lingering kiss to her knuckles.

Be still my beating heart…

"We still on for Bible study, then dinner later?" His voice was low and deep.

"Huh…oh yes…later. Absolutely."

"See you around, Lily."

He winked.

"Uh… You wish…Professor."

This time her standard, saucy retort came out a bit breathy, to her ears.

And this time it was her turn to stand, and stare, as he walked away.

As for just a moment, she quite literally forgot where she was.

Chapter 9

Romans 12:5
So we, being many, are one body in Christ, and
every one members one of another…

Lily knew precisely where she was.

Granted it was very dark, and the vantage point was a little unexpected, but she was definitely at a nighttime, outdoor Soca festival in Trinidad. The beautiful Caribbean Island her mum called home, and where she'd spent nearly twelve years of her young life before she finally settled in the US.

The temperature was warm.

The atmosphere was electric.

For certain, by the feel of it, she knew this would be one of those rare times when a dream was just a dream, and she got set to enjoy it. To bask in all the sights and sensations. To merely exist in that moment in time, in the nocturnal fantasy world being revealed all around her.

She inhaled deep and got a tantalizing hint of salt air, as a welcome ocean breeze cooled her heated skin.

Focusing on the sounds around her, she could hear the beautiful blending of musical instruments. The guitars, the keyboards, a host of brass instruments, and the unmistakable sound of sweet and perfectly tuned steel drums. All keeping in seamless synch with the deep rhythm of the base, and the fast tempo of the African Conga, and Indian Tassa drums.

Now, instead of being a spectator of a Carnival event, as she had been on so many occasions, she was up on stage, with the vibrant sounds of the band at her back. Looking out into a veritable sea of shifting human shadows.

"How yuh feelin'…?!"

Her gaze snapped to the right as a bright spotlight flicked on. It shined down on the lead performer as he issued his loud, guttural, yet melodic cry from a few feet away, and ahead of her. The very last syllable he uttered echoed around her head like a musical note at the end of a song. Lingered in the air, as he swung his thick dreadlocks to the left, then right, and pointed an index figure straight ahead. As though calling for only one single participant's response to his question. Even as an instantaneous and enormous roar of approval rose up from the unseen crowd beyond the stage.

"I wanna hear everybody say, yeah!"

"Yeah!" Was the screaming and overwhelming response amid thunderous applause. He bounded over to the left side of the stage in perfect timing with the building beat of the music coming from the band.

"One more time! On this side! Let me hear yuh say, yeah-yeah!"

"Yeah-Yeah!" The hyper-engaged audience on the left gave him an even more ear-splitting double affirmative to his request. With knees lifting higher and higher, he wasted no time in running back to the middle of the stage once more. He paused for a split second, looked back at her and winked. "Wha' 'bout you, yuh ready?"

The jolt of pleasure she got from that small acknowledgement unleashed an intense cascade of sensations unlike any she'd ever known.

"Yeah!" She screamed at the top of her lungs, then grinned.

"Well, all right then. One…! Two…! One. Two. Three. Let's go!"

The swell of the pounding rhythmic Soca music from the band grew to a pumping frenzy then, as he turned back, and faced the front of the stage. Then began jumping up and down with what seemed like boundless energy, and an even more enviable cardiovascular system. With a bright white rag in hand, he simultaneously sang and flung his hand up into the air over and over again. Waving the piece of fabric in perfect timing to the music.

"Jump…! Jump…! Jump! Jump and jump!

"Everybod–ay!

"Let me see yuh…!

"Wave…! Wave…! Wave! Wave and wave!"

Attracted by the vibrant and addictive energy he drew from the crowd like air into a vacuum, with the deceptively simple lyrics, she took one step forward and then a few more, until she stood near the very edge of the stage, looking down.

It must have been at least seven feet off the

ground. The feeling of excitement and sheer exhilaration held her in grip as she looked out into the electric darkness. Like watching an old movie go from black and white to technicolor bit by bit, and as though someone switched on a light, directly beneath her, the very front row of joyful, smiling, jumping, and gyrating patrons snapped into sharp view. Then the next row, and the one behind that one. A continuous wave of visual, and colorful energy moving outward for miles, thousands of people of every ethnicity rippled into clear view. All dressed in festive, colorful clothing. Jumping, dancing, and waving a virtual kaleidoscope of solid-colored rags, flags, and personal wrist drones in time to the music as though powerless to resist the siren call of the performer on stage as he issued his melodious instructions.

"It's amazing. Isn't it!"

She jumped as someone shouted near her left ear.

"Oh, dear God! Uri! You scared me half to death!" she shouted back over the din of the pounding music that was vibrating her body right up through the stage at her feet, on up to the hairs on her head, she imagined.

"Oh, sorry." His voice lowered as he snapped his fingers and the sound around them dropped to a conversation appropriate level. "I wanted to know how you were enjoying your little taste of home."

"This was your doing?"

He grinned.

"Well, of course it was." She returned his smile. "Who else could have orchestrated a dream this epic?

It's wonderful. I haven't been back to Trinidad for Carnival in years. I'd almost forgot how amazing it is to attend a Soca fete. And to see it this way? From the performer's perspective? It's literally mind-blowing. I've always wondered what it would be like, but never in a million years could I have imagined how utterly fantastic it is to be up on stage like this. Looking out at the crowd. The sheer spectacle. The energy. The people. It's electric. Thank you, so very much."

"You are most welcome."

"You know, I've always been in the audience, and thought how special the people up on stage were. And don't get me wrong I still think they're unique. It takes a different kind of individual to do what they do. Entertaining people day in and day out. It's only that tonight, I have a new appreciation for the audience and the very important role they play in all of this. Because none of this would be possible without them. Aside from the fact that there's no performance without the support of the patrons who come to the show, there's a kind of reciprocal energy. I actually felt it tonight and it was tangible. It's flowing up from the crowd out there, all the way up here to the stage. I can still feel it. Even now. I can imagine precisely how it would fuel a performer, giving them the impetus to keep going, and engaging, and connecting. I never considered until right this second how much both groups truly need each other."

"It's the way it should be. It's how you were meant to exist. In perpetual harmony with the Three in One, and with each other."

"I can't even imagine what that must be like for you. It must be phenomenal."

"That it is."

"I wish we knew how to live that way in the world we inhabit."

"You already do."

"Well, we're doing a really poor job of showing it."

"Oh, you only need to narrow your focus. Just as you couldn't run until you first learned to walk, you need to start with small steps."

"What? You mean in each country before we can do it across the world?"

"Think smaller. How you as an individual relate to the people you know. Many times, considering how, or what you say or do, can make a difference for someone close to you for instance. A kind word here or there. Taking their feelings into account and not focusing on your own. Or perhaps letting them know you value their opinion."

"So, wait…was all this intended to be some kind of lesson for me?"

"Hey, I'm here to create and enhance the experience. You take from this what you will. Every time."

"Hmm…" she considered his words and as he smiled that luminous, transcendent smile of his, she got a very real sense of the higher power at work. As in, the literal Highest.

"Now, are you going to stand there like a lump on a log, or are you going to show me how to jump and wave as a true-true Trini would?" He snapped his fingers and two white rags appeared in his hand.

Plus, the decibel level of the music returned to one that she could swear was making her kidneys vibrate.

"Oh, I don't think you're ready for this!" She snatched one of the perfectly sized rags out of his hand.

She grinned, grasped his right hand with her left, and felt a buzz of bliss like no other as she got set to grant his joyful entreaty!

Chapter 10

John 7:24
Judge not according to the appearance, but judge righteous judgment…

"Hey Lil. Wait up!"

She stopped and turned when Jake grasped her left hand, as he caught up with her in the hallway between classes.

"So, Jeri cornered me again. At the monthly staff meeting yesterday… Didn't you see her?"

"No. Why would I? And I should care about any of that because?"

"Aw, come on Lil." He gave her a cajoling look. "You have to help me out." He looked around and lowered his voice. "You gotta get her off my ass."

"No, as a matter of fact I don't "have to help you out", and excuse you? Language!" She glared at him. "You kiss your child with that potty-mouth? I expect better from you. *You…*" she levelled a schoolmarm look on him, "–should expect better, from you."

"Yes, ma'am," he eyed her, as his voice dropped to a velvety, yet grating rumble as he smiled.

Only Jake could make being both irreverent then repentant, seem so adorable and so hot, all at the same time.

"So, come on. Will you, do it? Can we make what we did the other day a 'thing', or what?"

"A *thing*?" She enunciated every syllable and let the 'G' ring at the end.

"Uh-huh. You know?"

"I'm not certain I do. So, by all means, enlighten me. Let's go back to my class for a minute. We can talk in there."

They turned and walked back towards the classroom she'd just vacated. She waved a hand near the door that between classes was set to open only from the outside with her biometrics, and those of the couple other teachers who also used the room. She ushered him in to stand where they wouldn't trigger the sensors that would reopen it for anyone inside wishing to exit.

"Okay, so exactly what do you mean by, a thing?"

"You know, you pretending to be my girlfriend, on a more prolonged basis?"

"I was afraid that's what you meant." She sighed.

"Hey, remember, you were the one who started this."

"Yes. But to save you. Remember that part?"

"Hey, I said thank you."

"Yes. Wonderful. You're welcome. Now does that gratitude make it okay for you to ask me to progress this charade even further?"

"Please? Just hear me out."

"Okay, I'm listening. State your case, Councillor."

"Well, for starters, she saw us on the quad this month. It'll be weird, if we're together one minute and then apart the next."

"No, it won't. People break up all the time. Next argument."

"Okay…uh…Oh, don't you think it's likely she'll assume she's the one who broke us up? After everything you said? She'll think she won… and at your expense. Would you be okay with that?" He eyed her.

Now, that one gave her pause. She wasn't at all keen on giving that daughter of Jezebel the opportunity to think she'd bested her.

She squinted her eyes at him.

"Okay, so that was sneaky, underhanded, and shameless–"

His eyes widened.

"…But still, quite brilliant really. Appealing to my vanity like that. You went straight for the jugular, didn't you? And so soon too," she rocked back on a heel, "I wasn't expecting that. Thought it would take you a while to bring out the big guns. Good for you!"

They both grinned.

"Now, I'm not saying that it is, but even if that were a valid assumption, me having such a fragile ego I mean. We're still going to get to that stage eventually. Why delay the inevitable?"

"That's exactly the point. It'll give me time to get out of her radar, while you get to ease out of the arrangement without her thinking she's got the upper hand. Plus, it'll only be when she's around the quad, or at faculty meetings, and as I said, only until I can get her off my…uh…case. Just until the…" he said something under his breath she didn't quite catch.

"Excuse me?"

"Until the semester ends." His words came out rushed, then he winced, as though he thought she might hit him.

"Wow, really?" She shook her head on a dry laugh. "Fine. No good deed, I guess. That is what they say."

"Great! Wait…what? Are you possibly suggesting that dating me equates to some kind of punishment?" His left eyebrow approached his hairline as the left side of his mouth quirked upward.

"Jury's still out on that one, Councillor. I'm sure I wouldn't know." She raised her brows and smirked.

"Uh-huh…" he gave her his slow smile.

"Okay, but if we're going to do this, I'd say we need to lay down some ground rules."

"Like what?" He sounded offended.

"Well, for starters let's talk PDA. There will be no capitalising on this arrangement to 'cop a feel.' That means no inappropriate touching or fondling, of any kind. Zero. And in case your interpretation of inappropriate differs from mine, that means you cannot touch me anywhere but my head, arms, and back, above the waist obviously. Oh, and no kissing on the lips. Also, you may return a caress, but *only* in like manner, and with a touch that is of equal or lesser intensity than the one I gave you. Understood?"

"Seriously?" He looked stunned.

"What?"

"You're kidding me with this, right? So, what? Is there a handbook on this out there somewhere that I'm not aware of?" He held his hands open and looked around as though expecting to be enlightened by someone appearing out of thin air at any moment. "And couldn't I just give you a kidney or something instead because I think that would be a whole lot easier."

She frowned as he chuckled.

"Oh, you joke, but it's important that we keep this straight and strictly…uh…straight."

"…Important…yes…" he nodded as he took a slow step towards her.

"Uh…because all it takes is one overly amorous kiss for show, and uh…" she noted his progress, "the next thing you know someone catches feelings and…uh…"

She completely lost her train of thought then when her butt connected with the side of the desk that was closest to the door. Not even realizing until that moment that she'd been retreating at the same pace as his slow advance.

An advance that had brought him within a few inches of her. She craned her neck up and met that intense gaze of his.

"One kiss."

"What?"

"I get to kiss you…once. On the lips. If the situation calls for it."

"What situation is that?"

"Oh, I think we'll know it when we see it." His mouth turned up in a slight smile.

"Well, uh–"

"And when it comes to how I can touch you…I just want to be clear. If you hold my hand like this," Without breaking their eye contact he reached out and took hold of her left hand, near her wrist, "would *this* qualify as a touch of an acceptably lesser intensity, as you said?"

She felt the light stroking of his fingertips down the back of her hand.

"Oh, well yes…I guess…that's uh…"

"Or…what about this?" This time the slow circling of his slightly callused thumb on her inner wrist took hold, and promised to do crazy-good things to her senses.

"…and about that one kiss…?" He continued caressing her wrist, and God help her, she couldn't summon up the will to pull away.

"But I haven't actually agreed to that. I mean, I haven't made up my mind…uh…yet."

"Yeah, yuh have." His head tilted to the side as he smiled.

"Well, yes, okay…but absolutely no Frenching."

"Hey, your loss…"

She watched in a near trance as his tongue darted out to lick his bottom lip.

"…Trust me… You haven't lived…until you've had my tongue in your, uh…mouth…Wait, what?"

She put a hand up to her lips to halt the projectile spray of saliva that would have escaped with the sudden outburst of a gust of noisy air from her pursed lips at his comment.

"What…did you just say?!" She burst into giggles as he joined in with his own hearty deep-toned laughter.

"Okay, so that did not come out the way I thought it would. At all. That was bad, right?"

"Awful, actually, is the word that comes to mind," she said around her laughter. "Oh, that was too funny. You should have seen the look on your face as the words were coming out. Like you couldn't even believe what you were saying, yourself. I swear, that was priceless."

"Okay, well at least it was good for a joke. I haven't laughed that much in ages."

"Me neither."

Their laughter faded and they stood there, enjoying the comfortable silence for long moments, she thought.

"So, it's settled. Terms of engagement set?"

"Yes. I should think so."

"Great." He turned and walked towards the door and she followed.

"Oh, and you owe me dinner for this, Professor," she poked his arm as they exited the classroom and paused in the hallway outside. "At month end. As soon as we get paid. Somewhere super fancy. None of that utter rubbish fast food, masquerading as high-end dining you enjoy so much."

He shook his head and laughed out loud again.

"You're on. Anything you want. And I'll have you know as far as dates go, you're looking at a winner. There's none better than this guy, right here." He jerked a thumb in towards his chest

"Oh, really? Tell that to barista-girl. What was her name again? Oh, that's right…you couldn't even bother to remember her name, could you? Since you decided to bail on your date last week."

She flashed him a grin as she started to walk backwards in the direction she'd been originally headed, and away from him.

"Oh, wow… Blind date-shame. Well, that stung." He shook his head. "I think I told you; she talked to one of my students after she saw me at the coffee shop. Between them they cooked up some hairbrained plan to set me up with her, which I did not agree to, by the way. That's the last time I tell you anything. Uh…" he clutched at his chest then pulled out a fake dagger, then grinned and winked. "See you around, Lily."

"You wish, Professor." She let out a squeak of a giggle. Then spun on her heel and sped up, as she rushed to get ready for her next class.

"Okay folks," she rushed through the door to her next class and placed her notetaker on her desk at the front. "Good afternoon. Please everybody, take your seats. We're talking about George Orwell's Animal Farm today, so let's get started. So, tell me…" she walked around to the front of the desk and leaned back on it, "What would you say if I told you, everyone is equal, but some are more equal than others? Come on. Anyone?"

"What my parents say vs how they actually treat me compared to my brother and sister," a voice in the back called out followed by a chorus of agreement from different people around the room.

"Ah, yes, the proverbial sibling rivalry. I can't say from experience because I'm an only child, but from what I'm told, the struggle is real. Am I right?"

A few chuckles and a group of voices among the two hundred or so participants were raised in solidarity.

"Okay, what else?"

"I think it's the tongue in cheek expression of an unrealistic ideal, really." Bradford's crisp British accent rang out. Not from his usual spot at the back of the class, but instead and not surprisingly from his new seat. Near the front. Right next to Katy. "Equality is merely a myth. Isn't it?"

"Okay, so now we're taking it to a-whole-nother place. I love that. Clearly someone just had a very productive session in one of Professor Traynor's philosophy classes." She smiled as he grinned.

"What do we think about what Brad said? There's a lot to unpack there."

"Well, on a philosophical level it made me think of the concept of moral relativism."

"Ah, another philosophy buff. How so Katy? Please, tell us what you mean by that."

"So, from what I've read, it explores the idea that morality isn't absolute, it's relative, based on your perspective. Whether that's of an individual, or an entire society. So, if that's the case, then it's like Brad said, equality's not real, or even possible. It's just an incredibly elaborate phony-bogus-baloney perpetrated on the unsuspecting masses."

"I'll tell you what's incredible, the fact that you

and Brad finally agree on something. Am I in an alternate universe right now? Or the *Twilight Zone* or something?" She grinned as the class burst into laughter. "Okay, don't mind me. I'm only messing with you two," she added as she saw them both give each other googly eyes and turn a bit red at her lighthearted teasing.

"But yes, you've both expressed valid opinions, and we could sit here and argue the merits all day long. The point though is should we be focusing on the illusive nature of the concept of equality, or is it more prudent to examine the motives behind any stated attempt to bring it about? Is it genuine or contrived? Socialist or self-serving? Think about that for a minute."

She paused to give them all a moment to consider her words.

"So, we've discussed one of the fundamental statements in Animal Farm and something integral to the story. Now, what's it about? In essence. What's the premise?"

"The dangers of totalitarianism?" Someone suggested.

"Yes certainly, and what else?"

"I think it shows the power of language. The way it can be used to manipulate and control."

"Precisely Luke, and do we see a link to a similar theme we saw in Macbeth? Yes? Remember we talked quite a bit about manipulation in our recent exploration, didn't we? Okay one more. What comes to the forefront of our minds when we dive into this Orwellian classic?"

"It's an allegorical critique of the Russian

communist revolution?"

"Wow, great job, Andy! That's as succinct a synopsis as I've ever heard. Come to the head of the class indeed. And such a good job from the rest of you as well. Thank God, so many of you have actually been doing the preliminary reading I assigned. Phenomenal!"

More smiles broke out around the room as Andy beamed.

"Yes, absolutely. In a nutshell it's a satirical picture of the particular political system of that time period. And no surprise, one that can fit any number of others since then and even today, that purport to represent all in society, when in actuality they're mired in hypocrisy and corruption. Where those in power twist and distort what is actually a self-serving concept of equity for their own benefit, and for the enrichment of those who bankroll their campaigns, or toe the line and support them.

"So, let's also think about so called leaders vs followers. It's a cautionary tale of what happens when you go along to get along and stop asking questions. Isn't it? So do we see any parallels today, in our present circumstances?"

Again, there were lots of nods and voiced agreement around the room.

"What the defenders are doing with that branding, and the fact that the administration is allowing it, is quite diabolical," Katy piped up. "We all think so. It's a blatant betrayal of the ideals they profess to stand for. Also, Ms. Kavanagh, we all wanna thank you and Professor Traynor for stepping up and starting those rallies against it like you have.

The members of the student guild here are joining with other universities, and not only here in NYC. We plan on holding a lot more coordinated, peaceful demonstrations to let our voices be heard around the country. Okay people?" She glanced back as the nods around the room became more numerous. "Fight the power!" She raised a militant fist and received a sudden uproar of cheers from all around the room.

"Wow...I'm so glad you shared that, Katy. I don't even know what to say. You are all taking a bold step, and I couldn't be prouder of you. All of you who are standing up for what you believe. In all likelihood it's going to be a long road. We're going up against a very powerful structure. Make no mistake. But always remember, you can do the wrong thing as much as you want, but almost never as long as you'd prefer. As history has shown, even the mightiest evildoers will eventually fall when faced with the might of those in the right.

"So, please be ready," she glanced around with her most reassuring gaze, "we may be facing a pretty nasty nightmare before we get to the rosy dream that's surely waiting for us on the other side of this."

Chapter 11

Proverbs 12:1
Whoso loveth instruction loveth knowledge: but he that
hateth reproof is brutish…

Lily opened her eyes to an all-too-familiar, nasty nightmare…

And to Jake. On her left…and in her head.

"Okay, so you have got to be kidding me. Is this some kind of macabre joke? Why on earth are we back here again?"

"No idea." She sighed. *"Come on. Let's try to get through it. The faster we get this bit over with is the faster we can get out."* She started to swing her legs over so she could step out, but he grasped her hand. Tugged on it until she turned back and met his blurry gaze.

"Is that all you can say? Really? Here we are, back in what is clearly shaping up to be the Groundhog Day, uh…night…from hell, and all you can say is, 'Let's try to get through it?' How is that possible? Am I the only one here who's freaking out right now?"

"No, you're not."

"*And?*"

"*And...to overstate the obvious, I've done this before, way more than you have, which means I know exactly how nasty things can get if you allow your emotions to get the better of you, to the point where you let your guard down and you're caught unawares. You should count yourself fortunate.*"

"*How do you figure that?*"

"*Because we're aware that none of this is real life. I can't even count the number of times I've been in the void and didn't know it. This place is deceptive. Sometimes I think I'm out of it and back in the real world, but I'm not, and that's not even the most disturbing part. It messes with your mind. It can cloud your judgement. Plant ideas in your head that you would never **ever** entertain otherwise. Make you feel like what you're experiencing is familiar to you. Ordinary. Even customary...and real. As real as everyday life.*

"*So, the best way to beat this is to keep a level head, and my experience has also taught me that the only way out, is through. Think of it as a very elaborate escape room. Like those mega five hundred companies' executives use at their super pricy strategic planning sessions. It's just a matter of figuring out what through means on any given occasion. So, go ahead and freak out if you need to, but can you please do it in silence, so I can think? Thank you.*"

"*Fine. Far be it from–*"

She glared at him.

"*Oh, sorry.*" It got quiet in her head at last as he held up his hands in a gesture of surrender.

"Okay," she took a deep breath in and looked up and around, *"there seem to be a whole lot more lost souls this time."*

"Really? Looks the same as last time to me."

"Hmm…that's odd… Anyway, strange enough, they're not near that same open door over there, so let's try that way again and see what we find."

"Okay, agreed." He shrugged.

She swung her legs to her right again and stood up through the passenger side door.

When he didn't immediately follow, she bent and looked in at him through the window.

"Today?" She spread her hands in a gesture of impatience.

"Showoff." He grinned at her. *"I can't get over the way you do that. I swear, it's the most awesome thing I've ever seen. So cool."*

"Wonderful. Thank you. Now, can you please get a move on."

"Okay. Hold your horses. You know I can't walk through things yet. Like you can."

*"Yes, but you **can** open the door and step out, can't you? Hurry up. That super-creepy one over there is starting to give me the stink-eye. Oh, and fair warning, if we go through that door and I see that carriage again, I'm going to run screaming in the opposite direction like an absolute lunatic. Just saying."*

He got out of the car and they went for the door. And just as before, out on the street, the carriage was indeed waiting for them, to their left at the curb.

"Yeah. No. So, that's not happening." She didn't scream or run, but she did spin away to their

right.

"*No, wait.*" He grasped her arm. "*Let's think about this for a second.*"

"*What could there possibly be to think about? Don't tell me you're actually considering climbing back into that thing? Have you forgotten what happened last time?*"

"*No, of course I didn't forget. I just think maybe…and hear me out here. Maybe, we could attempt the trip again, and try not to antagonize the, uh…*"

"*Oh, I see what's going on here. You blame me for what happened last time. Is that it? You think if it wasn't for me, your freaky little emaciated dragon would have, what? Carried you off into the sunset?*"

"*What? No, I–*"

"*Well, let me tell you, since it apparently bears repeating. You haven't been here as many times as I have, so maybe you don't know. This place is evil. Every single thing in here has been designed for, or has devolved, or regressed, or whatever, to the point where torture, insanity, mental anguish, and sheer chaos are the order of the day. Regardless of what, there are no pretty sunsets and happy endings in here. And the lost souls, even if unintentional, make it every bit as much of a horror show as the fallen do, for those of us living souls who are unfortunate enough to venture in here at night.*"

"*Okay fine, so what do you suggest we do then?*"

"*Don't. Don't do that.*"

"*What now?*"

"*Don't look at me like you'll deign to do what I*

want, knowing full well you'll hold it against me every second because you really think we should do what you want."

"What? No, of course not. What does any of that even mean?"

"I know when I'm being manipulated, okay? Stuart, my ex, he did that to me every single time he couldn't get me to do what he wanted, so trust me when I say I have a degree in spotting it from a mile away."

"Look Lily," he took in a deep breath and held up his hands, *"I promise you, that's not what's happening here. It's just as you said. I haven't been here as many times as you have, so I was only trying to suggest we take a moment to consider all the options. I don't know why, but I have this strong feeling the carriage was sent to us for a purpose. Which is the only reason why I wonder if it might not make sense to try it again, and maybe we make some different choices along the way this time. That's all I'm saying. But,"* he added, just as she got set to communicate her next thought, *"I also appreciate what you said about your superior experience in this arena, so let's do what you think we should do. Okay?"* He touched her arm and gazed into her eyes. *"Please."*

"Really?"

"Yes. Certainly. So, don't just stand there. Go on, lead the way, mon capitaine."

She started to turn away, even as his lips turned up in a quirky half smile, and he executed a near perfect salute.

She swung back.

"I'm kidding. I'm kidding. Just a little humor to lighten the…uh…moment." He cleared his throat.

"Uh-huh," she eyed him. *"Okay, so I saw a couple streets that way,"* she pointed to their right, *"let's go check them out, yes?"*

"Yes, sure. Just let me–

"Lil, look out!" He started to pull her out of the way, but it was too late, as in a split second, she watched the rear end of the same semi-truck from their first experience make an odd drift to the right, mount the pavement, and slam right into them.

Lily was drifting again.

Felt that odd tug and pull that she could never fend off, no matter how hard she tried. It carried her along, undeterred, even as in her mind she struggled and fought, and tried to mentally shake herself awake, out of its clinging grip, and back to her accustomed reality.

Last of all, she heard the end of her sharp intake of breath, in her head, as she jerked awake.

"Oh no…"

She was right back in Lucifer's Lambo… Again. For what was this now, the third time, in the space of as many months? What exactly–?

"Okay."

She jumped.

Again.

"So, I'm certainly no expert, as you've repeatedly pointed out–" the deep drawl in her head said.

She turned to her left and towards Jake.

"...but...correct me if I'm wrong because I'm guessing...this situation right here," he waved a finger in a circle above their heads, *"it can't be good. Am I right?"*

She sighed.

Chapter 12

Proverbs 22:6
Train up a child in the way he should go: and when he is old, he will not depart from it…

"Sam, I want you to meet my very dear friend, Lily Kavanagh. She's the very accomplished English lit professor at school I told you about, and my future wife."

Lily sighed.

Jake grinned.

"Oh, you wish Professor. Seriously?"

"Hey, you're the one who told me to break the ice I should introduce people with thoughtful details. I put a lot of thought into that."

"Thoughtful details are, 'she enjoys 3-D badminton and playing the e-cello in her spare time,' not an unsolicited matrimonial declaration. You really are a complete lackwit, you know that?" She giggled and looked up as she bumped him with her shoulder.

"So, you said."

He looked down…directly into her eyes and gave a low growl…for her ears only.

She took a step back. Looked away.

But still felt her face heat at the sound, and at the very private shared memory it so effectively brought to her mind with startling clarity. The humor. The silliness of it. The little jolt of unexpected pleasure. She recalled and felt it all over again…in the moment he'd just created for them both.

Like being cocooned in a small, secluded, and intimate room, she was transported right back to the very moment he'd labelled her playful scolding of him as 'dirty talk'. Cementing it in her mind as precisely what he said – their naughty little secret. For all time, and forever altering her every utterance of the word going forward.

Such a little thing and yet he'd turned the tables on her with such remarkable skill, she felt the slightest, almost imperceptible shift in their rules of engagement.

And to say she was quite unprepared for it, was an understatement.

"She's right you know, Dad. Pay no mind to him, Ms. Kavanagh. It's so nice to meet you," Sam extended a hand…attached to a social media firestorm of an arm.

Just one look at all the stylish and colorful, branded and bejeweled data dots, encircling and extending from her wrist to nearly her elbow, and Lily had no doubt that Sam was a young woman in the know. Replacing the jewelry worn by the wealthy in earlier centuries, these were as much of a fashion and status statement as a means of staying connected.

Although perhaps not as gilded, no youth of their generation, regardless of their social standing had less than three rows of the latest in communications tech denoting their affiliations. Sam had five. A fitting match for her trendy haircut and clothing as well.

"Oh, there's no need to be so formal." She shook the pretty young woman's hand for a brief moment, then pulled her in for a little hug. "Call me Lily, please, and it's lovely to meet you too Sam. Your dad has told me so much about you."

"All bad I'll bet." She grinned at him when they separated.

"Yes, well you really are the worst after all," he pulled her in for a side hug.

"Chip off the old block more like," she smacked his chest as she pulled away.

"Hey, watch it young lady. I can still cut off your allowance."

"Yeah, yeah."

She made a face at him as he pointed a finger at her and pretended to look stern before giving her a loving smile.

"Okay, come on, ladies, let's go inside and get our table, shall we? I made a reservation for us," he held out an arm to usher them inside ahead of him as the door they were standing in front of whistled open to allow them entry.

An android server came over right away to show them to their table, gave them welcome drinks, and then took their order of an assortment of Chinese food.

"So, what's the latest with you and Fearless? Courageous? Help me out here." Jake gave a dry chuckle.

"Dauntless, Dad, and don't even try that. You know his name every bit as well as mine. I really like this one." Her voice took on a musical note of pleading. "If you mess this up for me, I will kill you." She glared at him.

"No, you won't," he barked out a laugh. "I haven't paid for that summer trip you plan on taking with your chess club to Chicago yet, plus you love me too much."

"And I'm only going to Chicago because you won't let me go backpacking in Europe with my class. See Lily? You see what I'm dealing with? If you were responsible for an eighteen-year-old young *adult* daughter, wouldn't you let her live her dream of traveling around Europe?"

Lily laughed. "Hey, I'm staying way out of that one."

"Because you agree with me, right?"

"Excuse you? Did I stutter?" She let out a little laugh. "I believe I just said I have nothing to say on the subject."

"Anything could happen while she's there, and I'd be miles away. I'd be worried sick. Being away from home makes young people do crazy things. Come on, Lil? You must have an opinion." He opened his eyes a bit wider and gave her a look as he inclined his head ever so slightly in Sam's direction.

"Ahh… Okay, what I will say is, Sam, I think you need to consider the implications of precisely what you said."

"Huh? Which part?"

"Well, you prefaced your question with "if you were responsible". It's funny you should have used those exact words because that act of being responsible for another person is a weighty one. Your dad absolutely is responsible. For you, and in terms of his character. He'd do anything to keep you safe, so given the kind of person he is, I would think he takes that duty of care very seriously, wouldn't you?"

"Yeah… I guess."

"Exactly. Would you prefer he not do that?"

"Uh…no, of course not."

"Right again. Because you've come to rely on him to be there for you whenever you need him. You trust him? Trust his judgement?"

"Yeah. Sure."

"And is there anyone going backpacking in Europe that you've known as long, or trust anywhere near as much as you do your dad?"

"Uh…no, I don't think so."

"So, why wouldn't you trust him in this? That there would be a good enough reason why he doesn't think you should go?"

"Uh… well, when you put it that way. Wow… I guess I wasn't considering that point of view."

"See Sam. It's exactly what –"

"Hold on there, Professor. You asked for my take on this. Well, I'm not done. What about you and what you said?"

"What about me?" He looked like a kid caught with his hand in the cookie jar.

"In all the time that Sam's been away at university so far, has she ever done anything you'd consider to be crazy?"

"Well…no."

"So why do you think she'd be any different in Europe?"

"But it's much further away, and–"

"And that's just geography."

"And if you'd let me finish, I was going to say and what about the other kids' crazy quotient?"

"I asked Sam if she trusts you, so I'll ask you the same. Do you trust her?"

"Yes, fine. I already see where you're going with this line of questioning." He sighed. "You're about to say that I should trust that she knows better than to get caught up in any crazy behavior going on around her."

"No, actually I was going to say that because you trust her, you have to put some faith in your own assessment and conclusion, and how you arrived at it. You." She pointed at him. "Forget Sam for the moment. You can't let fear rule or cloud your decision. Not wishing it obviously, but any one of us could step out tomorrow and get hit by a low flying hover-cab. Anything can happen anywhere, and at any time. Which means you also have to trust that whatever the circumstances, we'll be covered by the grace of God to help us make it through. You have to let her live her life. You can't cover her in bubble wrap and lock her in the house. You get what I'm saying?"

"Yeah," they both responded, then looked at each other.

"I'm sorry if I was too hasty about turning you down with the Europe trip, honey."

"No, no, Dad. What Lily said made a lot of sense. I do trust you and if your gut reaction was that I shouldn't go, well then maybe I shouldn't. There's actually another trip coming up in the fall. It's only to one country and since I wanted to visit more places like the one this summer is going to, I didn't say anything about it. This one's to the Netherlands, and before you ask, the Red-Light District is not on the itinerary. It's a canal cruise and it's stopping at a whole bunch of famous sites like a new 3-D theme park, the Van Gogh Museum, and the uh…uh…I forget the name of it. It's this super amazing flower park. Supposed to be the biggest in the world."

"Keukenhof." He smiled and nodded.

"Yeah, that's right. How'd you know?"

"Someone mentioned it, so I googled it a while ago."

"Well, it's supposed to be amazing."

"Yes…it sure is."

He looked so serene and happy in the moment Lily wondered if he'd perhaps done that search while using his immersive VR gear. That look of contentment certainly hadn't come from looking at a mere picture, or a video on a screen.

"So, what do you think? Can I go?"

"A definite possibility. Let's talk some more closer to the time you'll need to book the trip."

"Yes!" She did a little shake and shimmy in her seat as she beamed at him.

"Hey, hey. Take it easy. I didn't say yes, yet."

"I know, but you didn't say no." She grinned.

"Oh great, I am starved," he looked up as their server returned loaded with fragrant dishes. "Not a moment too soon. Here comes our meal."

Lily glanced over at Jake as their android started to place dishes onto the table. Caught his mouthed "thank you", and nodded with her equally silent, "you're welcome."

"Everything looks so good, doesn't it? My turn to say grace, Dad?" Sam extended her hand and he grasped it.

"Lily?" She reached out with her other hand.

"That's so lovely of you, Sam, thank you so much." She held her hand and Jake's.

"Lord, please bless this meal…"

"Well, that was such a wonderful night out. Thank you so much for inviting me." Lily addressed both Jake and Sam after their dinner, as they stood right outside the restaurant talking, before they headed to their homes.

"Sure. And thank you for joining us. We've gotta do this again real soon." Jake smiled, then held up a forefinger and turned slightly away as his coms beeped. He tapped his wrist. "Hello? Oh, hi Tom. Can this wait? I'm out at dinner. Uh-huh…all right. Hang on." He turned back to them. "I've gotta take this call. It's one of my students who's struggling with some of the material I'm testing them on with a pop quiz tomorrow. Just give me a couple minutes."

"Oh sure, take your time."

He nodded. "Okay, go ahead Tom, I'm listening…" He moved away from them and started a slow walk towards the curb.

"Lily? It really was great meeting you tonight." Sam turned to her.

"I feel the same way. Both you and your dad are such a riot. I haven't laughed like that, and had this much fun in years."

"Me neither." She grinned. "Listen…" she glanced over to where Jake was standing still in deep conversation. "Would it be okay if I called you? I mean, to talk about stuff sometimes? My dad, he's great and all, but sometimes I feel like he thinks I'm still nine years old. Know what I mean?"

"Of course, you can call me anytime. I'm always up for a chat. Here's my info."

She held out her wrist so she could access the appropriate data dot.

"Wow…that is a gorgeous ring." Sam reached out and grasped the tips of her fingers. Tilted her knuckles up. "I noticed it at dinner, but seeing it now…wow. I know some people still wear jewelry, but I've never seen a piece this close up before. So intricate… What's it made of? It's beautiful."

"Thank you." She allowed Sam to pull it in even closer to her face as she peered at it. "It's a blend of several precious metals and stones. It's an ancestral piece. It's been in my family for generations. It's my mum's. Well, technically it's mine now, since she gave it to me when I was about eleven."

"Lucky you. The only thing I ever got from my mom was heartache."

"Oh, surely not. I know things didn't end well, but I'm sure if you think about it, you'll remember some good times. Didn't she ever take you out for ice cream when you were feeling low?"

Sam's sad expression was replaced by a slight smile.

"Yeah. We used to have some primo-epic ice cream breaks."

"There, see? And I'll bet if you try even harder there'll be even more lovely memories." She touched her arm, gave her an encouraging smile. "You just need to remember to be super thankful for those."

"I guess," she shrugged.

"It's like those famous words of Alfred, Lord Tennyson, an English poet of the eighteen hundreds. He said, 'Tis better to have loved and lost than never to have loved at all.' I think that's absolutely beautiful and so poignant. Wouldn't you agree?"

"Wow, yeah that's so real. I've never heard that before. Is that from the literature you teach too?"

"Sure is."

"I'm def gonna go check out the classic section of my e-library."

"You should. Lots of hidden gems and hours upon hours of jolly good fun." She grinned, then tapped her wrist to send the proximity alert with her info. "Oh, and you're preaching to the proverbial choir. I'm thirty-eight and my dad still treats me as though I'm in pigtails, playing cricket on the beach."

"Cricket? What's that?"

"Oh, it's sort of like American baseball, but not really. We played it in the UK and in the West Indies, when I was growing up. But as I was saying, that's the thing about parents, no matter how old you get, you'll always be their baby. I know you think it's inconvenient sometimes, but trust me, as you get older there'll come a time when you'll grow to appreciate the connection. If you nurture it, in whatever form it takes."

"I guess. That's what my dad says too."

"See? There you go, and he'd never steer you wrong. He adores you, more than you'll ever know."

"OMG! He told you that?" She looked over at him then shouted out. "Like creep me out, and get a life, why don't you?!"

"What? Can't hear you." He held up a hand to his ear, then grinned and pointed to his wrist to indicate he was still on his coms.

She made a face at him. He blew her a kiss then waved her away and went back to his call.

"And, you two are a lot alike too, you know that?" Lily shook her head as she smiled at their antics. "As much as you may think he's tough on you, he really gets you. I can tell."

"You think so," she rolled her eyes and sighed. "I guess."

But from her little secret smile, Lily could tell she was pleased.

Chapter 13

Psalms 37:8
Cease from anger, and forsake wrath: fret not
thyself in any wise to do evil…

"Okay, so let me get this straight. You think
it's the same semi that's been getting us every time?"

"Yes, I think so. In fact, I'm fairly certain."

*"But how? We got hit so hard. Every time. Plus,
it was super-fast. I know it's always some kind of
vehicle, but a couple times I don't think I could say
what hit us. What makes you so sure?"*

*"Well, on the back of it…you know? The end that
keeps slamming into us? One of the many
advertisements is for a cocoa mix called Sleepytime
that I enjoyed as a child during the time my family
lived in the UK. My mum used to joke that it all but
knocked me out, and made me sleep like a log. Thus,
the irony of what's happening does not escape me,
obviously."*

"You have got to be kidding me," he ran a hand
through his hair.

"I wish I was. I'm afraid this place is rife with

dark humor and bitter mockery just like that."

"Talk about adding insult to injury," he shook his head. *"Twisting such a pleasant childhood memory into something so awful. That's so sick."*

"Yes. Quite dreadful. So, between your Gruff the tiny starving dragon," she grinned, *"and my childhood cocoa nemesis, we've gotten ourselves into quite a pickle, I'm afraid."*

"A pickle?" He gave her a blank look. *"We're standing in the midst of a dimension that could mirror or rival any one of Dante's nine circles of hell and damnation, at any given moment. I'd say pickle is the understatement of the decade, wouldn't you? And is that dragon reference supposed to be funny?"*

"It certainly is. It's from that old song – Puff the Magic Dragon, remember that?"

"Yes, of course I do, and that wise crack right there, that was so unnecessary, I can't even tell you." His voice in her head sounded his agitation.

"Oh, lighten up. Having a bit of a chuckle about all this is precisely what we need to help us get through it, and almost guaranteed to confuse the socks off the fallen who I am sure are orchestrating all this. The last thing we want to do is to get all despondent and lose hope. That's exactly what they want. We'd be playing right into their hands."

"Okay, I get that. Maybe I'm a bit sensitive because that whole dragon thing is my fault."

She heard and felt the new note of sadness in his tone and got set to dispel it.

"Now that's utter rubbish. For whatever reason, we are in this together. And get ready because I expect we are quite likely about to be on the receiving

end of a world of crap because of me and my particular disfunction, so we'll be even." Grinning, she nudged him until she was satisfied that the smile he wore was genuine.

"*So, what's the plan this time?*"

"*Well, first off, I think we can agree we need to get out of this car.*"

"*For sure,*" he popped open the door and this time stepped out in the same time it took her to go through the passenger-side door. He came around to her side.

"*Woah! Look out for Public Enemy Numero Uno there,*" she pulled him a bit behind her and to the left as the lost soul who'd been eyeing them for quite a while was the first to separate from the approaching group and lunge at them.

"*Wow, thanks. I didn't even see that one.*"

Glancing over her shoulder a couple times to make sure none of them were following, she hustled them out of harm's way, and over to the open door. They walked through it and sure enough, there was the carriage waiting at the curb.

"*Do we dare?*" She turned to him as they paused on the sidewalk.

"*Well, it's not ideal, but I say we take our chances with our sometimes reasonable, sometimes not, lizard-dragon again. While we figure out what to do next. Misery acquaints a man with strange bedfellows they say.*"

"*They who?*" She couldn't quite contain her shock. "*Are you quoting Shakespeare right now? Or is that just me in my head?*"

"*Hey, if the situation fits,*" he shrugged.

"Since when?"

"Since I started taking an interest in classic literature, God help me." He chuckled. *"I think you're starting to rub off on me, Professor."*

"I highly doubt that."

Pleased nonetheless, she motioned to their waiting carriage. *"So, Gruff again?"*

"Absolutely, I'd take a bumpy ride and a mouthful of some seriously sketchy fabric, any day, over the guaranteed, almost immediate, and very unpleasant face planter from that truck. I swear I could still smell the exhaust from that dang thing for a couple minutes after I woke up last time."

"Yes, smells from this place are powerful, they do tend to stay with you. I remember once I had an unusual encounter in what I can only term as a hellscape. I've never smelt sulfur, but somehow, I knew that was the exact odor sort of lingering in my nostrils the next morning, whenever I got a flashback to that very intense experience."

"Wow…do I even want to know?"

"What?"

"The experience you mentioned. What it was about."

"No. Trust me. You do not."

"That bad, huh?"

"Worse."

His blurry countenance was a mix of concern and trepidation.

"Okay, so shelve that under the ever-growing list of 'you are officially freaking me out' conversations we've had so far. Never a dull moment with you, is it?"

"Oh, I'd love for us to be talking about dreams I had about class today, or my last outing to buy milk. Trust me. I'd trade all of this for a bland, vanilla dream experience in a heartbeat. Quicker than you could say Bob's your uncle."

"What?" He grinned. *"I've never heard that. Where do you get all those colorful expressions? I have to ask. They can't all be from the literature you teach, right?"*

"An inexhaustible e-library, right here," she pointed to one of the data dots on her wrist, *"21st century TV, of course, and it's becoming evident I have entirely too much free time on my hands to indulge in all of the above."* She returned his grin.

"Well, I am loving it. It's so much a part of what makes you, you."

"Thank you, for saying that. For quite a while there, I wasn't so sure…"

"What? What is it? You looked so sad for a moment there."

"I…uh… while I was with Stuart. I spent a lot of time examining so much of what I said and did. Trying to make sure it fell in line with what he considered to be acceptable. As I discovered over time, he had this vision…of what success should look like for him, and for whoever he was with.

"At first, it was only little things. Like – 'Is that what you're wearing?' or, 'Do you really think it made sense to say that?' Always so innocuous, nonchalant, and always phrased as a question, but I knew it was a signal to me to not transgress in that way ever again.

"Then it graduated to more significant

concerns, about when was I going to get a better class of friends? Shouldn't my chase for tenure be more aggressive? Or when was I going to get serious about financial management? You know? Growing my investment portfolio. Purchasing a house. A valuable asset. Instead of wasting money, month after month, renting an apartment. It got to the stage where nearly every word out of his mouth sounded like a veiled criticism of how I looked, how much I ate, who I associated with, what I was doing with my life." She rubbed a hand across her forehead as the memories came flooding back.

"I put up with a whole lot of rubbish...for far too long. You know, sometimes I wonder... would I still be there, if he hadn't hit me. I–"

"He did what?!"

The rage coming off Jake at that moment was palpable. She felt it vibrate the space around them for a moment. Having experienced something like it before, she hoped it was only in her mind this time.

"It's fine." She shook her head and touched his arm in reassurance, and tried to calm him down, as soon as she realized it wasn't merely in her head. She could actually feel the wave of his unabated fury begin to encircle them like a physical presence. She'd felt the ripples of her anger before, thrumming within and then spreading outward, like an unusual, exhilarating rhythmic vibration, at first.

Right up until what came next.

Something she hoped to never experience, ever again.

Because it felt like being at ground zero of a powerful explosion, or at the epicenter of an earthquake. All except for the noise. A cacophony of guttural roars, high-pitched shrieking, unintelligible shouting…and maniacal laughter. All ripping at her soul. Pulling it apart and away from its moorings. She'd never been quite so grateful to be jolted awake as she was on that particular occasion.

"He put his filthy hands on you?! In what world could that ever be fine?!" Jake's continuing and heated questions brought her back to their current jeopardy.

"I didn't mean him hitting me was fine. Obviously. I meant I'm fine now." She reached out to touch him again. *"Will you calm down, please? Your temper is causing a shift in the energy around us. Can't you feel it?"*

Maybe it was only in her imagination, but she felt a ripple of something go through her to him.

He paused for a couple seconds, looked down at her hand on his arm and then around.

"Yes…I can… What is that?"

"The fallen. I think. We may not be able to see them, but I think they're all around us right now. I can feel them. A whole lot of them. I think they feed off sin and negative energy like anger. Draws them to you like a magnet."

"And you're just telling me this now?"

"Yes. Because this is when it became relevant. I can't be expected to remember every single threat I've experienced and relay it all to you in one sitting."

"Okay, I get that. That's fair."

"Thank you." She spread her hands in an 'I told you so' moment.

"But don't think for one second I'm ever going to forget what that jerk did to you. He better hope we never cross paths. Ever. Because if I ever meet him, I'm gonna kick his–"

"Language..." she eyed him.

"Right. Sorry. But I meant what I said. There's nothing so loathsome as a man who would hurt a woman like that."

"It only happened once."

"Doesn't matter. That's still one time too many."

"Plus, it was the catalyst that made me wake up and realize I needed to end it with him right away. I might not have–"

"Don't. Don't do that."

"Do what?"

"Don't make excuses for, or justify what happened. None of that the end justifies the means, all's well that ends well, crap. You are an intelligent, sensible, self-confident, self-respecting, faith-filled woman. You would have found your way out, away from him, and back to yourself, regardless. He shouldn't have hurt you. Period."

"Well, thank you, for the vote of confidence, and for offering to be my champion. But I don't need you, or anyone else to fight my battles for me. As it happens, I've trained in martial arts, so a second later, when I recovered from the initial shock, I...uh...put him down, with a spinning back kick. I'm not proud of it, but–"

"Oh, yeah, you are." His face was set in determined satisfaction as he nodded and extended his fist. *"Come on now, don't leave me hanging."*

She paused, then bumped hers against his.

"That's my girl. Now that deserves an oorah. That S.O.B. had it coming. Yes, language, I know, but it simply had to be said."

"Would you believe he called later on? I think it was maybe two weeks later. Told me he had to ice his jaw for a week." She gave in to a little smirk, *"To get sympathy and to try to make me feel guilty, so I'd get back together with him, probably, but...I let him know that was never going to happen."*

"Good for you."

"Haven't seen him since."

"Good riddance."

"Yes... I guess..."

"What?" He turned her face towards him with a gentle finger beneath her chin. *"Don't tell me you're still in love with that reprobate even after what he did to you?"*

"Oh, no. Hell no. I don't even think I was in love with him to begin with. I just didn't want to be alone anymore."

"Well, what then?"

"I can't help feeling I failed somehow. Like I'm not enough. Just me I mean, the me without the labels, and ambitions, and expectations. That was my one and only serious relationship. Ever. And it took me a long time to get to that point after spending so much time trying to get me right. I've always thought that you need to spend twice as much time working on what you bring to the table as a whole, fulfilled person, than you do on looking for what you think you want to get from a partner. I dunno. Maybe I got it all wrong. Maybe I'm the one who maybe doesn't

know how to love."

"Now that's just straight-up baloney. You are one of the warmest, kindest, most unselfish people I know, and with so much to offer."

"You really think so?"

"Without a doubt."

"I know I probably don't say this enough so I want you to know how glad I am that we're friends. Having a guy that I can talk to about things like this, it's such a blessing. So, thank you." She reached out and touched his arm. *"I mean it."*

"Sure...uh...and don't let one bad experience make you doubt who you are and your value. The right person will arrive when you least expect it. Sometimes things just don't work out with certain people. People who aren't right for you, and sometimes that's nobody's fault. But then before you know it, along comes—"

"Like you and your ex-wife?"

"What?"

"I was wondering if that's what happened with you and your ex. That things just didn't work out."

"Oh... Our situation was...complicated."

He didn't say anything else, but she got the sense there was more to the story. A whole lot more.

"I thought I was going to spend the rest of my life with a man who turned out to be a Machiavellian narcissist who strikes women, apparently whenever the mood strikes him, pun intended. I think I can handle complicated."

"Look, this isn't the time, or the place, okay?"

"What?" She couldn't quite believe the vague words drifting around in her head. *"So, let me get this*

straight…you just grilled me on my nightmare of a failed relationship, but now that the shoe's on the other foot suddenly this isn't the time or the place? Unbelievable." She shook her head with a dry and humorless laugh.

"*Shouldn't we get a move on before we lose our ride?*"

"*Okay fine, sure. Why not? By all means. Let's get this show on the road.*"

They walked to the carriage. He helped her in and they were once again on their way at quite a fast pace.

"*Right. I say we look for the light,*" she suggested after a short while.

"*And I say I still have no clue what that is. Don't you think it would make more sense, and be a far more constructive use of our time to find a collaborative solution. You know? Maybe take advantage of both our perspectives? It's been some time. I think I'm quite seasoned at this now. Granted, not as much as you, but still. For instance, look at this.*" He reached up and snatched at a section of the dragon's turban cloth that had just whipped past her face. He pulled it down to their eye level. "*I noticed this the last time, but I wanted to get another look at it to be sure. See the detail in the stitching here? I think it's some kind of map, or maybe a code of some kind.*"

"*Are you being serious right now? Do you mean next to the ketchup stain right there? Oh, or wait, maybe below the spot that looks like it came out of the south end of Gruff up there?!*" She resisted the urge to roll her eyes. "*You have got to be joking.*"

"For Pete's sake, will you please look at it?! It doesn't appear to be arbitrary. Don't you think that section right there resembles some sort of a lettered code, and different from the fabric's pattern?" He pointed again.

"It looks like a mess, and utter rubbish is what it looks like." She made a rude noise in her head.

"That's because you aren't really looking at it as I asked. Would you just give it a–"

"I am too looking at it, and I'm telling you; you're wasting my time! We'd be much better off–"

"Oh crap...!"

"Wha–?"

It was the semi…

Again.

Chapter 14

1 John 4:9
In this was manifested the love of God toward us,
because that God sent his only begotten Son into the
world, that we might live through him…

"Again?!"

Jake grabbed a hold of the wall to his left as his head hung down for a couple seconds.

"Seriously Uri?" He glanced up. "I thought you said these lightning-fast transits of yours would get easier. I feel as though I'm in for a serious case of whiplash any day now if we keep this up."

"Actually, I didn't say it would get easier. What I said was you'd get used to it. There's a difference. And technically, whiplash is a neck injury. What you're experiencing right now is acute motion sickness, coupled with the effects of high G-force trauma."

"Well, thanks for the clarification, Doc. Now will you quit it?"

"And somehow…still…not your call. Correct me if I'm wrong, but haven't we covered this ground already?" Uri chuckled.

"He's right you know. He told us that first day when we…uh…okay." Lily stopped talking and compressed her lips when he stared her to silence, as with the aid of the wall, he pushed himself upright.

"And why are you so chipper? How come you're not feeling the effects of these jumps the way I am?"

"That's a good question. I don't know. I feel fine. Great actually! And look around…" she spread her arms wide, "we're in Venice right now. And it's Christmastime? Uri, am I right? Just look at all the beautiful decorations and twinkly lights."

She hugged herself as she felt the delightful chill in the air, and the tangible holiday spirit. In the distance she could hear the sounds of merriment, cheerful voices, music, clinking glasses, and intermittent laughter. Looked around at the staggering display of magnificent, multi-colored twinkling lights hanging from doorways and arches, looping along the bridge they were standing on, and all across the ones as far ahead as she could see.

"I can't believe it!" She gushed. "It's May in New York right now. This is incredible."

"You've been to Europe before. Haven't you been here already?" Jake gave her a curious look.

"No. I haven't. Have you?"

"Yes, I have actually. A couple times. Although not in the winter months."

"Well, good for you, Professor. This is my first time. Isn't the ambiance wonderful?"

She sighed as she leaned to look over the side of the bridge. Down to a two-passenger gondola, floating along in near silence in the canal directly below them. Even the boats were decorated. Their electronic lanterns bobbed in the fading evening light, and illuminated festive garlands, and glittering ornaments draped along their bows. "I mean look, those are *actual* gondoliers." She pointed to one of the men manning the boats. All decked out in a blue and white striped shirt, red neckerchief, and gobbo – the broad flat hats adorned with a matching ribbon they traditionally wore.

"Those are *actual* androids though, in case you didn't know."

"Nooooo…" She thought he was joking with her.

He nodded.

"Really?"

"Yep."

"Well, that's just tragic. When did that happen?" She felt her heart drop.

"About twenty years ago. Right around the same time they reopened for tourists. They had to hoist and shore up the pilings again to stop the Adriatic from swallowing the city. Where have you been?"

"I thought this was one of the few remaining traditions that wouldn't be broken down to just another human job that AI could completely take over and dominate. It's such a personal and special romantic experience. It's a form of art, I think. Their style of rowing, the way they sing."

"Well, sorry to burst your bubble, but these androids have got all that covered now."

"It's not the same though. Surely."

"So, still think the rough ride here was worth it?"

"I most certainly do. Besides, I don't experience

it the way you do. No doubt it's a turbulent re-entry to awareness, but I so love the excitement of it. Plus, I know it's Uri, so I know I'll be safe, and that I'm about to go somewhere I can't even dream of. Somewhere amazing, fantastic, and magical.

"Also, it feels different from being pulled into the void, don't you think?"

"Yes, that's true."

"And after what I've been through in that loathsome, scurvy hell-hole, as long as I wake up anywhere else but there, I am A-okay. Praise God."

"Hmm…" he had an odd expression on his face as he looked at her.

"What?"

"Here I am, quibbling over the journey, and there you are…delighting in the destination. I think there's a lesson in there somewhere. This trek of changing, evolving faith we take throughout our lives," his head shook from side to side, "sometimes we focus so much on the ups and downs, and how we think we should get there. Too much, maybe. When what I guess we should probably concentrate on is the goal."

"And maybe the goal isn't what you think." Uri added.

"How so?" Lily wondered.

"What would you say, if I asked, what represents that ultimate win? In your mind."

"Well, most would say heaven, right?" She got an answering nod from Jake.

"Sure. But that's just the construct though. A place. A way to simply and in a concise fashion define some-*thing* that's in actuality indescribable.

More correctly, I would say, it's some-*One*. Because it's all about connection, relationship, and togetherness on a level and to a degree you cannot yet imagine, or even appreciate for that matter. So, yes, by all means, strive for that finish line, but don't lose sight of why you're doing it in the first place. Live with love and gratitude in your heart, and with constant remembrance of the Three in One who makes it all worth it."

"Now that's really great advice, thanks Uri." Jake's expression was serene as he nodded.

"Absolutely, so useful and timely too." She felt the revelation he shared take root in her heart and mind.

"So, on to why I brought you two here. And it's not just because I know how much Lily wants to ride in one of those gondolas."

"Really? We'll have time to take a ride?"

"Of course, would I bring you all this way otherwise? I know it's on your bucket list."

She let out a little shriek as she grinned.

"So, let me get this straight… You still want to take a ride and risk being electrocuted if any water gets into the boat with one of those androids?"

"What?!"

He stared at her for a moment then his face broke into a broad grin.

"I'm kidding. They're perfectly safe."

"Oh, thank God."

"Or, at least I think they are, now. You know, since they put in those safeguards after that last very tragic incident."

She eyed him as he shrugged.

"You're enjoying torturing me, aren't you?" She crossed her arms over her chest.

"Immensely." He chuckled.

"See? This is precisely why you can't handle it when Uri gives us a snap D.I.E.T."

"Really?"

"Yes, I said it."

"Oh, now why would you go there? That was harsh."

She smirked at him, then returned his smile.

"So, can we take that ride now?" She turned back to Uri.

"In a bit." Uri nodded, his face solemn. "First, I need to tell you that in a little while you're going to be visited…by someone."

"Who? The ghost of Christmas decorations?" Jake barked out a laugh.

"Unbelievable. Will you please let him finish." She tried to glare him to silence. "And must you be so irreverent? Have some respect. Uri is one of God's blessed messengers. You can't speak to him like that. He's not one of your school chums."

"Oh, come on, you have to admit, given where we are, that was funny as hell," he said, still laughing.

"By Jove! And there you go again. Funny as hell? Really?"

"What? Come on Lil. It's just an expression. I didn't mean anything by it. Uri knows that." He turned to him. "Right? You know that. Right? Don't you?"

Uri regarded them both. Looked from one…to the other…and didn't say a word.

She glanced at Jake and wondered if her face

reflected as much trepidation and holy fear as his suddenly did. She felt her breath catch. She held it.

Right up until Uri burst out laughing, "Of course I do! I'm just messing with you. You should have seen the look on your faces." He turned to Jake, "That was so brilliant. A Christmas Carol, right?"

"Uh-huh…" Jake still looked like he might pass out at any second.

"I saw that. I get it! So many of your more obscure and less popular entertainment references go right over my head, but I actually got that one! And you're right. That was so funny. Just priceless." He continued howling. "I haven't laughed like that in a while. Ah…so good.

"Okay, so let's walk along this way," he gestured with a hand as his laughter faded. They moved off the bridge and onto one of the little lanes on one side. "So, as I was saying, someone's coming to meet with you. He'll come find you, so don't be alarmed if he kind of pops up unannounced."

"How will we know it's him? What does he look like?" Lily wondered.

"Oh, he's kind of hard to miss. And if I know him, he'll announce himself in his own, shall we say…peculiar way." He grinned. "Verndari call him Budbringer. He used to be their press liaison, between them and the human population. But what they don't know is that he's one of us, one of God's original, true messengers. He's been infiltrating their ranks with Godly purpose for some time now. He can tell you whatever you need to know about Verndari to advance to the next stage of the conflict. Help enhance the part you'll both play as individuals, and together, as you guide and mold young minds so they aren't led astray during this perilous time."

Jake let out a little whistle. "I know we talked a bit about this before, but it sounds like a very tall order the way you say it. You sure you've got the right people for this plan of yours?"

"Absolutely. You're more than up to the task, so don't even worry about it. Besides as long as you remember who's got you, nothing is impossible. And all things work together for good to them who love Him and are the called according to His purpose. Amen?" He beamed.

"Amen." Lily echoed his words and mirrored his smile.

"Okay, so here we are. Right on time." He held out a hand to show them a gondola as it floated up and docked near to where they were walking.

Excited beyond measure, Lily moved in closer to the boat.

"Okay you two, why don't you go on ahead and enjoy the ride now, hmm? We'll talk more once you're done with it."

"You're not coming with us?" She stopped and looked back as Jake stepped in then took her hand to help her get into the bobbing boat.

"These babies are made for couples. Squashing my frame in there with you two is def not my idea of a good time. I'll sit this one out. But don't worry. I'll be around. You go on. Enjoy yourselves. You can put your heads together, and see if you can't come up with some ideas for what else we can do to make this next rally a true stand-out. Among other things..." his brows popped up right before he disappeared with a smile.

"Huh? Other things? Well, that was cryptic." Lily wondered about his comment. "I mean there's only so much more we can do at this next rally given it's scheduled for tomorrow."

"Yeah, but you know Uri. What a card. Am I right?" Jake cleared his throat. "So, what do you think about us using those new electronic, 3-D info bombs, with the targeted messages?" Jake helped her sit on the warmly blanketed bench, then settled in beside her.

"Um…okay. Sure. I think it could actually be a good idea."

"Buon Natale! I am Alberto. Welcome to Venice." Their gondolier who'd been watching them board the boat, greeted them with a cheery tone.

"Oh, thank you, so much, Alberto. Merry Christmas to you too!" Lily beamed.

"A song perhaps, for you two young lovers tonight, yes?" He said in heavily accented English.

"Oh…uh…no, we're not–" she started to shake her head, even as Jake said, "Young?" He gave a dry chuckle as he shook his own head.

"Certamente, signore. Amor non conosce travaglio – Love…it never tires. It is timeless, yes?"

"What a beautiful sentiment… Grazie. That was lovely, truly it was. But still, can we maybe enjoy only the experience of the boat ride?" She turned to Jake. "If that's okay with you? Would you mind terribly if we sat back and soaked in the ambience and the quiet of the night?"

"No, sure. That's fine by me."

"So, thank you so much, but no song tonight.

Maybe another time?" She smiled at the gondolier.

"Ah…molto buono. As you wish, signora." He turned his back to them and began rowing them at a smooth pace through the canal.

Enjoying the ride as they sat in comfortable silence for long minutes, she started to take note of various subtle patterns in the ornaments hanging from the bridges and in the archways they passed.

"That's so extraordinary."

"What is?"

"See the decorations there?" She pointed up to one set on the left, "And even up there," she gestured to the bridge directly above as they drifted under it. "Look at the way they're clustered together. I swear every time I look; I see a different shape. Hearts, doves, swans, roses, cupid, even padlocks in a pattern like the ones I've seen couples attach to the Love Lock Bridge in Amsterdam. Don't you see it?"

"Hmm…maybe." He looked around.

"Well, I think it's all positively glorious." She sighed in pleasure as she relaxed and absorbed the entire experience as they continued to glide along.

"Wow, you're really into this, aren't you?"

"Huh? How do you mean?"

"It's just the sublime look on your face. I can tell how much you're enjoying this."

"You have no idea. I've read so much about what it's like to be here at Christmastime. I've always wanted to visit. It's much quieter so it's such the perfect time for a gondola ride. It's so magical, isn't it? Listening to the oars cutting through the water. That soft swish, and lull, and swish again. It's like listening to the liquid version of a melody. So soothing and therapeutic."

She shifted her leg. "Okay, so these really are cozy, aren't they?" Perhaps she hadn't noticed until now, but suddenly there didn't seem to be enough room for both of them to sit without touching. She tried and failed, a couple more times, to keep her thigh from pressing against his wide spread one in the close quarters of the small boat.

Perhaps it was only in her over-active imagination, but aside from his long, sturdy leg, she fancied she could also feel the heat of his arm that was resting behind her across the stern. It seemed to surround her, fending off the bracing chill in the air, and the feeling was… Well…

Surprising…

"You can relax your leg, yuh know."

"Huh? Oh, right." She gave a nervous laugh. "I…uh…" she looked down. Straightened the very pretty patterned skirt she only just realized she was wearing. Gaped at the stunning, gorgeous matching heels on her feet.

Wow…

"I promise you…" Jake's soft rumble interrupted her shoe fixation. "I'm well vaccinated against another Covid outbreak. I don't have any social diseases, and I don't bite… Well, unless of course you enjoy that kind of thing. In which case, I'm sure I can accommodate you…on occasion."

"What…?" Her head snapped up and around. "Uh… No…of course not. Uh…why would you even–"

She caught his slight smile.

Then, both felt and saw his face, inching closer

and closer in the dim light. She pulled her chin into her chest so far, she thought her neck would pop.

Was he trying to kiss her? Surely not.

He raised an eyebrow.

"You and your jokes. Don't be silly. That's, uh…not what…"

His head tilted to the side.

"I…uh…" she started to protest again, then felt a little giggle burst out as she received his full, quirky smile last of all. "Oh, I'm such an idiot, aren't I? I'm sorry. I'm a grown woman and we've been friends for months now. Why do I feel so nervous sitting like this?"

"I don't know. You tell me. Why do you think you're so nervous?"

"Well, when I was with Stuart–"

"And here we go." His sigh was heavy. The chill she felt due to his sudden retreat, keen. As he pulled away from her, as much as their confined space would allow. "I wonder, do you think we could ever have one conversation of this nature, without you comparing me to your creep of an ex-boyfriend?"

"What does that mean? There's no comparison. We're not together, Jake."

"No, we're not. You're so right about that. And this back and forth we do? Talk about whiplash. I think it may be even worse than the D.I.E.T. jumps. I am so done with this dance," he mumbled then gave a dry laugh.

"What are you on about? That doesn't make sense. I don't understand what's happening right now."

He leaned forward. The shaking of his head from

side to side was slow. Pained. He looked down.

"What? Will you talk to me, please?"

"It's nothing to concern you. My mistake." He slapped his thighs. Ran his hands along them almost to his knees. "Are we done here?"

"Done with what?"

"This boat ride. Because if you are, we should think about finding Uri."

"Well, okay, but I don't see him anywhere." Still a bit unnerved by his sudden odd, matter-of-fact manner, she tried to search the faces of the people on the bridges above for Uri's familiar countenance, as they approached them. "Should we ask the gondolier to dock somewhere? How do we even get out of here?"

"Beats me." He sighed and leaned back. "He normally just appears. Maybe we should–"

"Had enough?" Their new gondolier, Uri, turned back to look at them. His face somber as he uttered his question.

"Quite." Jake rose from his seat even before Uri had them docked at a nearby mooring spot.

"Where'd you come from? How long were you steering the boat?" She sounded her alarm as Uri's clothing made a rapid shift from the gondolier's garb, back into the casual shirt and slacks he was wearing before. He helped her disembark right behind Jake.

"Not long. I thought you two could use a little privacy. I only popped back in a minute ago when you mentioned me."

"Oh…" was all she could think to say. Still utterly confused by the exchange she'd had with Jake.

"Why so glum?" He slapped Jake on the back, then winked at her. "Not to worry. I imagine tomorrow is going to be quite eventful. A blessed and glorious day for you both. Trust me."

He grinned.

Chapter 15

Colossians 3:23
And whatsoever ye do, do it heartily, as to the Lord, and
not unto men...

"I say…it's a most blessed and glorious day for a rally, isn't it?"

Lily spun at the sound of a deeply toned British accent reminiscent of her father's, even if a smidge more upper crust!

There, in the bright afternoon sunshine, approaching her from a couple meters away was a body like nothing she'd seen outside of Uri himself and his miraculous D.I.E.T.s.

Well, hullo Chris Pine's, charismatic Captain Kirk…meets Alan Ritchson's, rugged Reacher…meets her very favorite 'late forties-ish, hot guy with a British accent' fantasy.

Only, taller…more muscled…and way hunkier…

And dressed in a chest-hugging, soft, white shirt, casual black slacks, and very expensive-looking loafers.

Ooo-la-la, indeed…

"Just the perfect temperature out here as well. Don't you think, Lily? Warm, but still cool enough so one doesn't have to suffer the indignity of perspiration pooling in all those decidedly unmentionable places."

He beamed at her and she wondered if it was only in her imagination that contrary to his conclusion, it had suddenly become a bit *too* warm outside.

"Budbringer, I presume?" She held out a hand and looked up, when he stopped right in front of her.

"For these particular intents and purposes."

She thought his answer curious, but then forgot all when he took her hand in a strong warm grip and shook it. Leaving her with the same feel-good sensation she always got whenever she touched Uri. Only different. Somehow. She was distracted from pondering the exact nature of the distinction when she noticed something else.

"Hang on a second. Where's Jake?"

Grateful again for the fantastic turnout, she looked around the area of the massive grounds of the university where they were standing. She tried to peer in between the throngs of people. With an assortment of 'BAN THE BRAND' electronic placards hovering over their heads. Chanting slogans and setting off circular rings of info-bombs off and on within their designated groups. They'd even managed to garner the attention of reporters from some of the leading media houses. In fact, she was pretty sure she caught a glimpse of Pulitzer Prize winner Dax Newton a couple minutes earlier.

"That's so strange. Jake was here a minute ago.

Can't think where he's wandered off to. Let me see if I can find him." She tapped her glasses, intending to hit him up on his coms.

"That's okay. There's no need, just yet."

"Huh? But why? Aren't you here to share some of your expertise with both of us on how we can ramp up this, and future rallies?"

"Well, yes and no."

"You know, has anyone ever told you that for a messenger of God you're quite cryptic?"

He gave a dry chuckle.

"Well, I'll tell you what, over the epochs and ages of time, I've come to find that sometimes the best way to get people's attention so you can share something important, and often times not what they expect, is to – one, get them to answer their own questions, and two, keep them guessing so they stay engaged."

"Well, then I'd say you're off to a positively ripping start."

"Ah…this one's got that fire! Ha! Ha!" He threw his head back and laughed even harder. "And such wit. I like that." He eyed her. "I can see why he loves you."

"Who, God?" She beamed, anticipating his response, given his obvious connection.

"Uh-huh. Him too." He smiled back with a chuckle and she completely forgot what she'd planned to say next.

"So, uh…anyway. Where should we start?"

"Well, anywhere you prefer. Though at the beginning is always best. Tell me about you." He pierced her with a gaze that went right into her.

"Whatever you feel comfortable sharing."

"Oh, okay. Well, I'm a professor here at the university, as you probably already know. I love teaching. I actually transferred here from California some months ago, so it will be a while before I can even think about getting back on the track to tenure. But that's okay because English literature is so much more than what I teach, it's my passion. I simply adore fiction. Particularly the classics. Of course, some may say those who can't do, teach. So perhaps I do live vicariously through the literary works I inhale, a bit." She chuckled. "Uh…sometimes. But, other than my work though, I'm trying to be more focused on my spiritual walk right now. I don't need to tell you obviously how important that is. Of course, I'm nowhere near where I need to be, so I've got some ground to cover. Let's see, uh…family means everything to me too. I try to see mine as often as I can. You know to be really present. Although sometimes I still feel I should do more…" she paused as she noted his half smile, "uh…is there anything…uh…anything else you'd care to know? Any question you want to ask?"

"Mm-hmm…quite a few, actually. First off, how long do you intend to keep selling yourself short like that?"

"Excuse me?"

"Do you realize that every single positive statement you made about yourself was swiftly followed by either a detraction, or a disclaimer?"

"Uhm, no not…" she tried a mental recap. "Really?"

"Oh yes. It's insidious, isn't it? At first, you tell

yourself you're merely working on your flaws because that's what people do. They try to be better. Right? So, you can be new and improved. That better you. More approachable, more physically attractive, more tolerant, more generous, more fun, more dynamic, more irresistible. More..."

His head tilted to the side as though he was considering something. "Particularly for when that special person comes along... Yes?"

She felt stripped bare when in that very instant, his eyes went from piercing, to soul appraising.

"But then, before you know it, years have gone by and the list of things that need tweaking and fixing grows, becoming virtually insurmountable. You're questioning your self-worth, and wondering if you'll ever be good enough. For anyone… No matter what you do..."

Completely unbidden, she felt her eyes tear up at the veracity of his words.

"Ah beloved…when will you learn?" He reached out with a gentle touch. Brushed away a single tear that escaped to roll down her cheek. "I'm here to remind you, lest you forget, you were made precisely as our great Creator intended. In every jot and tittle. Every nuance and expression. Every quirky trait that makes you, you. Including your extraordinary skills."

He gave her a pointed look that was telling.

He knows…

The thought rippled through her mind. She froze. Wondering what she should say. But there was no need she realized, as he continued.

"Why not inhabit your peculiarity in this time

and in this place. Embrace it! Then turn within. Not to self, but to Him. The giver of every good gift. Exalt Him. Celebrate Him and what He means in your life. The perfection you chase is quite literally impossible. Why not be the best perfectly imperfect, unique you, that you can be, instead? Why not perform…for an audience of One. It will be a far more productive and rewarding use of your time. I promise you."

"Thank you, so much for that." She nodded with a smile. "I think I got more from what you just said than from a month of all of that high-priced therapy I've done in the past."

"You are most welcome. Ah, and right on time, here's Jake now."

As he said, she saw Jake navigating his way through some of the nearby protestors.

"Ms. Kavanagh?"

She turned in the opposite direction at the mention of her name by one of her students.

"Yes, Andy?"

"What should I do with this next batch of refreshments?" He was carrying quite a large crate.

"Oh, leave it with me. I'm about to head over to the south side to see how things are going over there. I'll take it to them. Just give it here," she held out her arms. "Thank you so much Andy."

"Sure, you're welcome." He beamed, handed it to her and hustled away.

"Hey, hey, hey! That looks super heavy. What were you thinking? Let me take that for you." Jake rushed over and relieved her of her burden. "I'll go get a floating trolly so we can move it to wherever you want it to go." He squatted down to place it on the ground near them.

With massive arms crossed over his chest, Budbringer leaned down to her and said right near her ear, "Haven't told him yet that with your strength, you could *literally* snap him like a twig, have you?"

"No, of course not."

"Huh? Did you say something?" Jake stood to his feet.

"Oh, uh…look who's here." She waved a hand in Budbringer's direction as he all but melted her with a dazzling grin.

"Let me guess…Budbringer?" Jake extended his hand.

"In a manner of speaking." He winked at her, then shook Jake's hand.

"Okay, wow…that was just like Uri…only different."

"You noticed that too, huh? He's different all right." Lily smiled.

"Hmm… So, you had a chance to talk already?"

"Oh yes, Lily and I have been getting along quite swimmingly. I'm positively chomping at the proverbial bit to have a chat with you both, now that you're here."

He beamed, looked at each of them in turn, as his eyes took on that luminous soul- building brightness, she'd witnessed firsthand.

"I'm Gabriel by the way. Talk to me, you two. I'm listening…"

Chapter 16

Ephesians 4:32
And be ye kind one to another, tenderhearted, forgiving
one another, even as God for Christ's sake hath forgiven
you...

"Lil, will you just hear me out?"

"Okay, fine. I'm listening." She sighed.

"Look at this end of the cloth. Right here." He pointed at the same section of the scruffy looking fabric he'd shown her the last time they'd found themselves in the void together. This had to be at least the seventh time. But at this point, who was even counting.

"Look at the design in the stitching."

"This, again?" She resisted the urge to growl in utter frustration. *"I already looked at it, and I told you; there's nothing there but schmutz, and food stains, and rubbish."*

"Now look beyond that, will you, please? Really focus on this part of the pattern that doesn't match the other."

"All right fine," she huffed. Already planning to stare and nod with an, "Oh yes, that's so interesting,"

to appease him, she grabbed the end of the material out of his hands.

"Okay, see? I'm looking at it. Yes, it's interesting, and sure, these may look like letters, but…wait…what…?"

"What? What? Do you see something?"

She saw something all right…something she hadn't noticed before.

"Wait just one minute…" She gazed down at the intricate looping of thread. Stared at it as a vague memory from long ago came rushing back with startling clarity.

"You know, I think I may actually recognize this. When I was a child, my dad used to join us sometimes when my friends and I played at being cops and robbers, and MI6 agents. And whenever we played spy games he came up with this super fun one where we used a Caesar shift cipher to make and then decrypt coded messages we'd send to each other. I haven't seen it in years, obviously, but I think I can read this. We were kids so my dad made it really easy for us. If I remember it correctly, and I'm right, each letter here will be two letters before the intended one. Let's see…it's in a kind of spiral pattern, but this looks like the first letter grouping here, on the left in this bit of the cloth. It's a G, I think. Then the next one is an O."

"Wouldn't that be 'go', then? As in, shall we at last go get the heck on out of here. We only need to figure out which direction is out, I'd say. Sounds like plain old English to me." He chuckled.

"And I considered that when I looked at first, but the next letters are, 'RM'. See? That make any sense

to you, Professor?"

"Okay, point taken."

"So, as I was saying, the G would be an I, and the O–"

"A Q, right?"

"Exactly." She smiled as she sensed his excitement and satisfaction over their unexpected progress.

"Although there's a space after it, which would seem to indicate it's a two-letter word."

"IQ? But that doesn't make any sense."

"Hmm… It could, depending on what the rest of it says."

"Let me take a look." He held onto one end of the cloth. *"I definitely see the G, but are you sure about the next one?"*

"Yes, I'm fairly certain it's an O. Here, hold this end a bit straighter for me."

She tried to stretch the fabric out some more herself when it seemed he wasn't helping and was trying to peer at the piece he was holding instead.

"Will you please hold it steady?"

"And I'm trying to, but it's not easy. The ride's getting really bumpy again for some reason."

"Well, it looks to me more like you're trying to look at the pattern yourself, rather than holding it steady for me."

"Because…if you must know, I think you're wrong. Dead wrong. To me that looks a lot like a D, not an O. Which, by the way, would make more sense. When's the last time you had your eyes checked, Professor?"

She heard his dry chuckle in her head.

"Is that supposed to be some kind of wisecrack about my age?"

"No, of course not. I–"

"My eyes are perfectly fine, thank you very much. And perhaps you need to remember which one of us is actually qualified to teach English. To accurately interpret and then convey the sometimes subtle, but most times very obvious nuances of the language." Irritated, she smirked at him.

"Really? I cannot believe you! That's because of the other day, isn't it? Because I didn't know it was comic irony that Shakespeare used the phrase 'Comparisons are odorous', instead of odious?"

"Not surprising at all, since your grasp of Shakespeare quite literally stinks!"

"Well, excuse me for breathing, Professor high and mighty, queen of everything Shakespearean! Not everyone is like you–"

"Oh!" Lily awoke to her sharp cry of pain as she felt the impact of the truck right down to her bones this time. She felt it. In very real and lingering anguish. Unnerving. Terrifying. And in an entirely new way.

Because this time, neither one of them had even seen it coming.

"How is this even possible?"

She jumped at the sound of Jake's deep voice above her head.

"Hi. Good morning. I didn't even see you come up." She tapped her wrist to shut down her electronic newsfeed. Then sat up straighter on the bench she was sitting on, out in the university quad, and tucked some loose strands of her hair back behind her ear.

"Sorry. I didn't mean to startle you."

"It's okay."

"And about what I said…"

"No need. I'm sorry too. That wasn't us. That place brings out the worst in people I think."

"Peace offering?" He held out a hand with a trendy, brightly decorated hot drink cannister.

"Is that tea?"

He nodded.

"Earl Grey?"

"Is there any other kind?" He smiled.

"Oh, bless you." She practically snatched it out of his grasp and returned his smile as she shifted to allow him to sit beside her on the bench. He took a drink from his own cup.

She raised hers to her lips. It had the perfect amount of cream and sugar, with just a hint of lemon.

"Ooo…so good. Thank you." She took a larger swallow.

"You're welcome. I figured you could use a bracing cup."

"Mmm…oh, yes. Exactly what I needed after the night we had. Or should I say morning."

"Which brings me to the point I was making when I walked up. How can it be that it felt as though we spent hours in the void in only a fraction of that time, huh?"

She shrugged. "The way time passes in there is very different."

"I turned in late, well after three because I had to finish a lesson plan, and when I checked my bedside clock after we got hit by the semi… Again. It wasn't even 4 AM. I am exhausted right now. How are you doing?"

"Same. Plus, it doesn't help that I didn't go back to sleep. I stayed up trying to figure out what I could remember of the coded message."

"And?"

"And nothing."

"Yes. I tried to remember it too, but I'm drawing a complete blank. It's like that section of my memory got completely erased."

"I hate to say this, but I think we'll have to wait until we're in the void again to get another good look at it to try to figure it out."

"Oh, you have got to be kidding me." His sigh was deep as he ran his fingers though his hair. "If we get hit by that truck one more time, I think I'll lose it."

"I know exactly what you mean. And for what it's worth, I'm sorry I didn't listen to you sooner about the pattern on the fabric."

"It's fine. I imagine the normal rules of logic and basic sanity pretty much go out the window when we're there. Plus, things don't look or mean the same for me as they do for you. I don't know how they're different, but they simply are. Don't ask me how I know. I couldn't even begin to tell you. I feel it. Every time we connect. In our minds. It's weird."

"Yes, exactly. You noticed that too? It's as though we're together, but it's also that we're still each on our own separate journey in a strange way."

"Maybe that's the problem? Maybe we need to have more of a meeting of the minds?"

"I don't see how. From the moment we woke up in that car we disagreed about how to handle practically everything."

"Oh, come on. That's not true. We agreed about a number of things."

"Oh, really? Name one thing."

"Uh…"

He shifted a bit on the bench. Looked at her. Opened his mouth…then shut it again. He looked straight ahead and took a sip from his cup.

"Dang, we're gonna grow old and gray in there, aren't we?"

"Uh-huh…most likely."

She mirrored his pose and drank her tea.

Chapter 17

Ephesians 3:16
That he would grant you, according to the riches of his glory, to be strengthened with might by his Spirit in the inner man...

"Like this?"

Trying to mirror the strong, yet graceful pose of her sensei, Lily planted her feet.

"Yes, now stand tall, and keep your shoulders back a bit more. Feel your center of gravity." He reached out. His touch to the middle of her back gentle but firm, to correct her posture. "That's it. Try to tap into the power surging up from your core. Now once again, with me."

Taking in a deep breath, she began to perform a series of precise, coordinated movements right alongside him, and in front of her mirror. An intricate and graceful kata that had been handed down through innumerable generations.

Stepping forward and then back, she bent her knees and squatted low, with arms outstretched, she let her wrists lead the way, as he'd taught her. First making large circles in the air before her, with the heels of her palms thrusting outward. And then again, with the backs of her hands instead, with thumbs tucked under. Balancing her weight as she shifted to the left and to the right, from side to side, all while she extended her legs, feet, arms, and fingers in elegant, slow sweeping arcs.

She tried to ignore the beeping of her coms then, but the sound became even more insistent.

"Hiko-San, I'm so sorry, please, give me one minute. I need to take this." She faced him, pressed her right fist against the open palm of her left hand, at chest level. Signifying God's powerful sovereignty, met with acceptance and openness. Then bowed, in their time-honored tradition. He matched her action then rose again, tall and strong.

Each time she saw him she couldn't help but be taken with his unusual, rugged good looks. Straight hair as black as a raven's wing, and with a streak of bright silver here and there, hung all the way to his shoulders. He had such kind dark eyes, slanting up at the sides and hinting at his Asian ancestry. All wrapped up in an easy smile, and a quiet, self-assured manner.

She stepped to the side, bent to retrieve her towel, then dabbed at the perspiration on her face and neck. She slung it over her shoulder, then tapped her wrist. "Hello?"

"Don't trust him." The male voice on the end of the line was strange. It sounded scratchy and stilted, and as though it was digitally altered.

"What did you say?"

"You heard me."

"What? Who is this...?"

"Do you seriously think he'll be any different?"

"I said…*who* is this?"

Hiko touched her arm with gentle fingers, his eyes filled as always with concern and compassion.

"I can sense your agitation. This distraction…it has disrupted our connection. Perhaps we should continue our session later, Lily-San?"

"Uhm…yes, okay. Arigatou," she inclined her head in a subtle mark of respect.

Hiko bowed low and she watched as his three-dimensional form collapsed downward and disappeared in a bright white circle at the spot where his bare feet had been.

She returned her attention to the call, "Now, I asked you a question. Who is this, and how'd you get my number?"

"Not necessary. What's important is you better watch your back. Your *friend* is not who you think he is. Don't believe him. Don't be manipulated again…or you'll wind up just like her."

Beep.

"What? Like who? Hello? Hello?" She tapped her wrist and heard nothing more.

She tried the call back feature on her coms, but still got nothing but crickets.

How very odd…

She looked up from her wrist. Stared at her likeness in the mirror ahead of her for a moment…and as it began to change.

Mesmerized, she took a single step forward. Watched, as the room surrounding her in the reflection was replaced by a rushing blackness. An instant before the glass began to crack and splinter.

She screamed. Raised her hands up to protect her face. As it exploded. Sending countless shards of jagged projectiles her way.

"No!" She awoke with a violent jerk, still screaming, and with arms and legs flailing.

And shaking, in abject terror…

Because she could still feel the sharp bite of the glass.

And because the feminine reflection she'd seen in the mirror…wasn't hers.

Chapter 18

Romans 10:17
So then faith cometh by hearing, and hearing by the
word of God...

It couldn't be...

Surely either the reflection in the plate-glass window she was looking at, or her eyes were deceiving her because she could swear the person across the street coming out of the Food for Thought shelter right then was Stuart.

After promising for months to get together with Melanie, she'd gone there to visit with her, and as soon as she exited the ultra-modern building, she noticed a new shoe store right across the way. She'd run across the street and stopped to look in the window, and there behind her...

She spun around at the very instant that he looked across the street.

"Lily!" He waved, hustled to cross through the traffic, and made his way over to her.

He looked...different. Thinner. His clothes were mismatched and nowhere near the expensive quality she'd been accustomed to seeing him wearing. And more than that, he looked so tired, and much older than his age.

"I thought that was you leaving the shelter. God, you look amazing."

"Thank you... Wow, Stuart...is that really you?"

"In the flesh, so to speak." He tried a small smile that didn't quite succeed.

"Oh...wow...you look... I mean what are you even doing here in NYC?"

"Long story." He gave a deep sigh shook his head, looked down at his feet, then back up at her. "Do I look that bad?"

"Uh...no...you look fine. You just seem different from the way you did when I last saw you, that's all. Plus, I wasn't expecting to see you. You startled me, that's all."

"It's okay, you don't have to pretend for my benefit. I could see it in those beautiful, expressive eyes of yours. The minute I came over here. A combination of shock and pity."

"Oh no, surely not."

He laughed then. Genuine and unexpected. It burst out of him. She'd missed that laugh. Forgot how much she enjoyed hearing it. And with it the tiniest twinge of regret resurfaced within her for what could have been.

"Oh, how I've missed hearing you use those words. You always had such a quirky way of saying stuff."

He sobered in an instant. Looked sad again.

"Well, I guess you got me good, huh?"

"What? Are you saying this somehow happened

because of me? Some kind of mystic karma that you always talked about?"

"No, of course not. And I don't follow that kind of stuff anymore. I think you must be happy to see me get mine like this. That's all," he shrugged and looked down at his feet again.

"Look Stuart, I know we didn't end on good terms, but you have to believe I'd never derive pleasure from seeing you hurt. Seeing anyone hurt. I made peace with what happened between us a long while ago. I forgave you. To release you and for my own peace of mind."

"And I realize that it's me who should be apologizing to you. Treating you the way I did. Letting you go was the worst mistake I ever made, Lily, and not only because of what happened to me. I see that now, so clearly."

"What exactly happened to you?"

"I left Cali and came to New York, thanks to a promotion from my old job. It was soon after we broke up and…well…my whole world fell apart. I met this woman. Said she was an investment banker, and she was amazing, or so I thought. Beautiful, brilliant, great in bed, and with a real head for business. She introduced me to this new hybrid venture capital hedge fund. Told me it was all the rage with the big power players on Wall Street. She got me to invest a little, and I hit the jackpot. I mean I more than tripled my investment, so naturally she convinced me to put in even more." His eyes filled with sudden tears. "I gave her everything I had, Lily. Even took out a second mortgage on my new place here in NYC because I thought it was such a sure thing."

"Oh no, Stuart," she felt an answering wetness gather in her own eyes.

"Yuh know…" He sniffed. Pinched his nose. "I've heard stories about people being swindled, and I always thought they must be the dumbest idiots to get suckered in like that. Right up until the morning it happened to me. I tried to call her to clue me into how things were going. To get some preliminary figures. But her number was discontinued. Went over to the bank where I thought she worked, and they'd never even heard of her. She'd always met me outside on the curb, or someplace else. I was so stupid I never even noticed I'd never actually seen her at work.

"So, of course, by now I'm in full panic mode because I know this can't possibly end well. I went to the police. They tried to track her for a month or two, but they said the trail ran cold. They couldn't find any trace of her so they said they'd keep in touch. Let me know if they ever found anything. Meanwhile, I was ruined. I was so obsessed with what she did to me and since the police weren't helping, I used every opportunity to chase every lead I could on my own. No matter how vague, or how much of a long shot. Someone called and said they thought they saw someone matching her description, I dropped everything and went there. I couldn't focus on work, so pretty soon I lost my job. My house. Then most of my friends. It's a slippery slope that gets you to this place.

"At first, I survived sleeping on a couple friends' couches, but after a week or two you start to get the message that you've overstayed your welcome, yuh know? One minute I was a successful corporate strategist with everything going for me. Everyone's go-to-guy. Then in the next I had an empty bank account, was a literal pariah among my friends, and homeless on the street.

"Well, thank God, eventually I lucked out. Found out about the Food for Thought shelter, so I had a place to sleep, and I could get a meal when the odd jobs I was doing didn't provide enough for the day.

"The woman who runs the shelter, Elise Sharpe, she actually saved me from making the biggest mistake of my life a couple months ago. It was a low time for me. I was all over the place. Physically and mentally. In and out of the shelter. I'd made up my mind to go to the Verndari Center to get implanted. You know, the one right down the street from here? Well, she happened to be there that day. She convinced me and a bunch of other people who were waiting to go in, to not take that hellish brand. She got me to come back to the shelter instead. She gave me a whole new lease on life, and clean clothes, and eventually a job."

"Wow…that's amazing. It's a good thing you didn't do it. That brand is a death sentence. People simply don't know it. I'm so glad you dodged that Verndari bullet."

"Yeah, you and me both…

"Listen, I know what I did to you was bad. Really bad. I still can't believe you found it in your heart to forgive me, but since you have…well…maybe…I mean…I'd love for us to start over."

"Oh…I don't know Stuart…" she shook her head.

"Just as friends of course," he hastened to add, "No pressure. I've got my new job at the shelter. It's going very well. I'm rebuilding my life and I know this will surprise you, I joined a church and I'm working on my faith, like you always tried to encourage me to do. I see it now. Everything you tried to tell me. Everything you tried to get me to see. The importance, the power and the comfort of faith. It's real and I finally get it."

He smiled. And it was the most genuine and heartfelt one so far.

"Well…that's just wonderful Stuart. I'm so happy for you, but I–"

"No. Don't shoot me down yet. Please… Just promise me you'll at least think about it?"

Taken in by that smile and his pleading gaze…she relented. "All right. Listen, I've got to get back to the university. I'm running late as it is."

"Of course. Sure. It really was great seeing you, Lily."

"Same here. You take care, Stuart."

And as she walked away, she couldn't help but wonder, was this what that crazy dream, slash, weird intersection with the void she'd had the previous night was about? Stuart? Trying to start up some semblance of a relationship with her again? Clear out of the blue? She didn't believe in coincidences. It had to mean something, her meeting him again.

Do you seriously think he'll be any different…
Don't trust him…

The eerie stilted words came back to her, echoing in her brain like the direst of warnings.

Chapter 19

1 Corinthians 12:4
Now there are diversities of gifts, but the same Spirit...

Don't trust him...

As though summoned, the whispered words invaded her thoughts yet again for the hundredth time that day.

Lily shook her head to rid it of her unwanted visitor taking up real estate, and looked across the campus walkway to distract herself. At the other benches scattered around, and at the nearby grassy knolls. Noticing as she did that absolutely no one was having any kind of face-to-face interaction with another human being.

Every single one of the young people, and the few teachers she saw as well were all alone. Completely absorbed with their personal tech. Some of them sitting fairly near, but still not facing each other or connecting in any way.

"Ever wonder what people from the last century would think of how absorbed we are with our tech nowadays? I know they were glued to their laptops, tablets, and cell phones. But think of how we've progressed. Everyone in their own little virtual world. Talking and interacting with someone, real or made-up, through their glasses, or VR headsets. Someone no one else can see. Can you imagine what we'd look like to them?"

"Yes, like absolute lunatics," Jake said around a bite of his sandwich.

"Probably." She snorted with a laugh. "Little by little the need for personal interaction is slipping away. It's amazing what you can get used to, isn't it?"

"Yes, it is. I remember how I thought I'd always be having Sunday dinners with my wife and kid, and instead when she left, I had to learn to do it all on my own. True I don't cook, but I still had to clean up after us, all while keeping Sam entertained, and engaged. Help her do her homework, and get her all packed up and ready for school the next day."

"Wow, that must have been difficult." She held the straw from her drink to her lips and took a long pull of her cold, fruity drink.

"You have no idea. Nothing but the grace of God got me through those first few months. Then I got some semblance of a rhythm going. Eventually, even started to find a sense of fulfilment and enjoyment in the time we spent together." He wiped his mouth and fingers with his napkin.

"So, your wife, she never tried to stay in Sam's life?"

"Uh…no. Once she'd made up her mind she wanted out, she was completely out."

"Wow, I can't imagine abandoning your flesh and blood like that. It's inconceivable to me."

"Well, that's because you've got a strong moral core, and a meaningful faith in God, so behavior of that nature wouldn't sit well with you."

"No, it wouldn't."

Wondering how best to broach the topic of his mysterious wife, she took the opening offered.

"So, uh…your wife…she didn't? Have a meaningful faith, as you put it?"

"No… No, she did not."

"Did something happen along the way to make her lose faith, or was she always that way?"

"She never had much use for religion, or spirituality, or any of that."

"And you were okay with that?"

"No, but I married her anyway." He sighed. "Guess I made the ultimate ego move thinking she'd change…for me. Instead, she got worse."

"Oh, wow… How so?"

"Uh…listen…you finished with that?" He pointed to the remnants of her lunch.

"Yes."

"You feel like taking a little walk around the quad, before we go back in? It's such a nice day out." He grabbed up their garbage and rose.

"Okay. Sure." She rose as well and waited till he dumped everything in the nearby trash receptacle and returned to her. He started walking and she fell into step with him.

Realizing from the change in his demeanor that she was hitting a brick wall with her current line of questioning, she changed course.

"So…by the way, I had the strangest episode in the void the other night. I wanted to mention it to you to get your impression of what I experienced. First, I dreamed I was having a session with my sensei, and then–"

"You have a sensei?" He turned to look at her.

"Uhm…yes. You remember, I told you about how I defended myself from Stuart that night?"

"With that sweet flying back kick?" He smiled and nodded. "Still so good."

"Yes…if you say so," she smiled back and shook her head.

"Well yes, of course I remember. But when you said you knew martial arts, I figured it was from a kickboxing class, or something like that. So, which discipline do you train in? Karate?"

"Yes, among others."

"Which ones?"

"Uh… All of them."

He stopped walking. Barked out a laugh.

"Okay, very funny. Where's the hidden camera drone," he looked around with a grin, "because you must be pranking me right now."

She pursed her lips and shrugged.

"Holy…" he ran a hand through his hair and stepped back. "You're serious?"

She nodded.

"What the…? I don't even know what to say. Since when has this been a thing with you?"

"Well, I've been learning a multitude of skills since I was about eleven. Fairly basic stuff until I was a bit older. Then I started to receive coaching in different martial arts and combat techniques. Along with uh…strength and endurance training. For a while now. Naturally I don't talk about it. You're the only person I've ever told."

"Wow. Not sure if I should be honored, or scared by that."

"It's fine. You're fine," she waved away his concern.

"It's a very ancient art called Aisuru Senshi – The way of the beloved warrior. It's a blending of disciplines, if you will, along with some other ah…unusual spiritual gifts."

"That is so amazing. I've never heard of it. Not that I'm familiar with any of the Asian arts, anyway."

"It's got a rich history. Conflicts conducted with dignity and honor. In the early centuries a group of elite warriors used it to defend kings, princes, and noblemen. They were actually in great demand in Asia and Europe, for their unparalleled skill in combat and artful subterfuge. It's something handed down in my mum's family for generations. Normally to sons, but well, her dad only had her, and she only had me so…" she shrugged again as she wondered about his expression. "What?"

"What, you ask?" His brows rose for a brief moment above wide eyes. "I got nothing. Frankly, I think I'm still in shock. It's not every day I find out my best friend is some kind of super-secret ninja, and probably knows a handful of ways to kill a man."

"More than a dozen, actually."

His brows popped back up.

"Uh…but who's counting, right? And I'm not any kind of ninja. Don't be ridiculous," she gave a dry chuckle. Waved away his concern. Again. "At most, I'm stronger than I look, and well, the lethal force is all a part of the teaching. Sure. But this is a different time. Other than what happened with Stuart, which was instinctual, really, I've hardly ever used what I know. As far as I'm concerned, it's simply a fabulous way to stay in shape, and in touch with God."

"God? Is that right? How so?"

"Well, a lot of what I've been taught is faith-based, and about staying centered and tapped into God's grace and power. Legend has it that the uh…special ability that each of the warriors had, was a gift from Holy Spirit, not unlike the gifts we've read about in the Bible, but it's only that they were able to tap into their full awesome power potential and connection to God."

"Wow, that's amazing. So, what's your gift?"

"No clue. Think it may have skipped a generation," she gave a dry laugh. "My mum has this uncanny wisdom and discernment. Sometimes she'll share a vision, if she's led by the Spirit, and it is always spot on. Even with me for instance. While I was growing up, she always knew what was going on with me, even when I tried to hide something from her. But me…? Nothing. Who knows…? Maybe one day I'll figure it out."

"I have no doubt you will."

They both turned and started walking again, almost by mutual unspoken understanding.

"So anyway, I was telling you about my freaky dream?"

"Oh, right. Go on."

"Well, I was training in front of the mirrors in my exercise room and I got this call on my coms. I answered and this very strange male voice was on the other end saying things like, "Don't trust him," and that I'll get manipulated again, oh, and that I'll end up just like her."

"What?"

He stopped walking again. His question was sharp. "End up like who?"

"That's exactly it. I have no idea what any of that meant. And then the mirror completely shattered. I mean it literally exploded in my face. I've been terrified before, but I'll tell you, that one took the cake. It's strange… I can recall the sharp bite of the glass hitting my skin, and the strange male voice, clearly. But I think I saw something, or someone, standing there within the mirror, right before it shattered. But I can't remember that part. I've been running it through my mind, over and over. I don't know what it means. Well, except maybe about the 'him' I shouldn't trust…"

"Look, I know what you're going to say. I–"

"So, you think it's about Stuart too? Right? I knew it." She reached out and grasped his arm for a second. "That's the other thing I was just about to tell you. I saw him, this weekend."

"Wait, he's here? In NYC?"

"Yes. Small world, right? I went to visit a friend and I met him on the street right after. He told me such a tragic story about how he got swindled and lost everything. He's working at the shelter on 42nd Street now. Can you believe it?"

"Crazy world…"

"You're telling me. So, he wants us to be friends again."

"You have got to be kidding me. The nerve of

that guy." He turned away a bit then turned back. Rubbed a hand through his hair. Put his hands on his hips. "What'd you say?"

"He made me promise to think about it…"

"And…? Lil…? You're not seriously considering being anywhere near that guy again, are you?"

"No. Of course not." She shook her head then faltered.

"Lil?" He grasped her arms. "Look at me…"

She met his concerned gaze. Watched his eyes dart left and right as they searched hers.

"Once an abuser. Always an abuser. Come on now."

"That's not true. People seek help all the time to learn to control their violent proclivities."

"And he's gotten himself some help? Is that what you're telling me?"

"No. I don't know. The only therapy sessions I know about are my own. Once we were done. I cut ties."

"And with very good reason. Stay away from him Lil. Heed the warning," his gaze shifted a bit. "Please."

"Okay. All right."

She pulled away from his touch and started walking again.

"So, a shattered mirror, huh?" He caught up and looked her way.

"Yes. It was awful."

"Well, you know what that means, don't you? Seven more years of crap luck in the void."

"Oh, no. Surely not," she sounded her alarm. "I

feel as though I've barely survived the last two as it is. Anyway, I'm not superstitious like that."

"You sound like Sam, right after she spills some salt, and right before she throws a pinch of it over her shoulder 'just in case', when she thinks I'm not looking." He chuckled.

"How is she anyway?"

"Oh, she's fine. I think. Kids grow up so fast nowadays. She's away at university and I hardly ever get to see her. Makes me so glad I got to be with her as much as I did during that critical time when she was growing up. I felt I was doing something of real importance then."

"And you still are."

"Hmm…sometimes I'm not so sure about that. When she needs something sure, but the rest of the time," he shrugged.

"Oh rubbish! I've seen the way she defers to you. Always asking your opinion. She thinks the world of you. Anybody can see that. She gets a little frustrated when she thinks you smother her…a bit," she added when he gave her that 'dad look' she knew only too well from her own father. "Look, I was planning on telling you, she calls me sometimes, I hope that's okay."

"Of course, I was hoping she'd reach out to you. That's part of the reason I wanted us to get together for dinner as often as we do. She won't say it, but I know she misses having a woman to talk to. And since her mom, well, there hasn't been anyone that I let into her life. I didn't want to take the chance that anyone would hurt her. She's been through enough. It was so hard for her to let go back then. She struggled so much. Now she's older I think she needs a positive influence. Her girlfriends are like her. Green. Young and inexperienced in life. She needs guidance from a strong woman who can teach her what it means to handle and express all that amazing feminine energy and power she's growing into, and not get taken advantage of, or taken for granted. I'm so glad she can turn to you to teach her how to shine, like you do."

"Okay, wow. You think I shine?" She felt a broad grin spread across her face.

"Without a doubt. You are luminous."

"Oh, stop."

"No, I'm serious. You're an amazing woman, Lil. I count myself blessed every day to have you in our lives."

"I don't even know what to say…well…except for – Nice try, Professor. I'm still not having the S.E.X. talk with her for you. No matter how much you try to flatter me." She nudged his arm with her shoulder and grinned.

"Really? And here I thought I got you for sure with that last compliment. Well, you can't blame a guy for trying." He returned her grin. "But, seriously though, I meant every word I said. You are an ideal role model for any young woman. Intelligent, self-assured, poised and classy, and strong in your faith. Plus, you're a phenomenal teacher."

"Thank you. It means so much to me to hear you say all that."

"Tenure, can go hang. You should be extremely proud of what you've accomplished so far."

"As should you."

"Just look at us. What a pair, huh? See? I keep telling you, we've got it all."

He reached out a fist and she bumped it, with a smile, and without a second thought.

Chapter 20

Proverbs 27:12
A prudent man foreseeth the evil, and hideth
himself; but the simple pass on, and are punished...

"Okay, *that's it. I think we've finally got it*
all this time."

She nodded as she followed the spiral of letters
as he read them out.

"GD... See? I told you that was a D, and not an
O."

"Yes, fine, I'll alert the press and drone your
medal out to you in the morning. Can we get on with
it please?"

She heard his little chuckle in her head.

"Right so it's...
GD RM UGL WMS BYPC
RFGQ WMS KSQR
GR QRYPRQ UGRF R
YLB CLBQ GL BSQR.

"So that's I and F. Uh...T...O. Then W...uh...
Geez... This will take forever."

"No, it won't. Hold it steady and let me do the
translation bit. I did this a hundred times as a child."

"Okay, be my guest."

"Right...let's see...

If...to...win...you...dare," she took a few moments to translate.

"Um...

This...you...must...

Okay, I think that's right, for the first two parts."

"You know, I have to say, just like you and your Slumbertime mix–"

"Sleepytime."

"Same difference." He waved away the distinction. *"Like you and your cocoa mix, the irony of this whole thing isn't lost on me. It's sort of funny when you think about it."*

"Funny? Really? I can't wait to hear this one," she glanced up from the fabric.

"Think about it. This stinky piece of cloth has been smacking us in the face from day one. Exactly the solution we've been looking for, all this time, and it was right there. Quite literally in–"

"In front of our faces. I get it. Not sure it's that funny though. How about we laugh about it after we've actually beat the maze, huh?" She straightened out the section of the material she was trying to translate.

"Okay, right. What about the rest of it?" He helped her.

"Let's see, the rest says...

It...starts...with T

And...ends...in...dust."

She looked up into his eyes.

"And ends in dust? You sure?"

She nodded. *"T-dust? Is that a thing... Some*

new drug...?"

"No, it's not. What the heck is that supposed to be? T-dust isn't even a word." He let go of the end of Gruff's scruffy turban, and it almost immediately started whipping around on a brisk breeze like a thing possessed. *"That's almost as much of a riddle as the code was."*

She heard his heavy sigh in her mind.

"Okay, so let's think about it for a minute. It must be something that turns dusty over time, right? And starts with a T."

"So, what? Like trash?"

"Hmm...if to win you dare, this you must...trash. Trash what though? No, that can't be it."

"I agree. What about T-words. Uh...turf, or terrain? Like dirt. That can be dusty."

"No. It says 'If to win you dare, this you must', which indicates we need to do something. Those are both nouns. We're looking for an action. A verb. You were on the right track with trash, but now we just need to find the right verb."

"And then what? We keep riding in the carriage till we get an opportunity to do whatever it's suggesting?"

"I don't know. Maybe? One step at a time though. We haven't even solved it yet. Let's try to do that first, then see what we come up with after."

"Well, since lately we seem to be able to remember the code once we're out, we could actually wait and see if this is one of those rare days where we just wake up. Without getting our faces slammed by a truck. Then we can sit in the quad, in more comfortable and normal surroundings, and

brainstorm over breakfast."

"But we're here now. Why not strike while the iron is hot. We may see something that might trigger...uh...something."

"See what Lil? The back of the semi? Because other than traffic on the highway, and the dodgy roadkill out in the middle of nowhere, that's about the only thing we've seen in months, and that's only when we've managed to make it away from the dang curb."

"I disagree–"

"Well, of course you do."

"What's that supposed to mean?!"

"Aww hell..."

That morning, he brought her two of her very favorite cherry and cream cheese filled tarts. A perfectly lovely pairing with her cup of Earl Grey.

Chapter 21

Psalms 66:10
For thou, O God, hast proved us: thou hast tried us, as
silver is tried...

"Thanks again for the breakfast pastries this morning. They were *so* delicious. Your best apology yet, in fact." She grinned. "Thank you." She looked up and nodded as their android server deposited their drinks on the table.

"Yes, well. I figured I owed you. Big time. Ah..." he looked down at the electronic menu rising out of the table in front of him, "I think I'll have the shrimp and chicken pasta, please. Oh, with extra parm. And the lady will have...don't tell me... The parmesan chicken salad. Am I right?"

"Yes, thank you."

"Oh, and put some extra honey mustard dressing on that as well for her, will you please?"

"Very good sir," the server nodded before rolling away.

"Right again. Well, just look at you. Acing the friend test all the way, aren't you?" She settled her napkin in her lap.

"Thank you. I try." He grinned. "Plus, you're incredibly easy to order for. But I have to say, you're missing half your life not having the pasta here though. It's the best in the state. I'm telling you."

"Oh, this restaurant looks like a cut above the rest, certainly." She looked around at the décor and high end finishings. "But best in the state?" She pursed her lips, "I don't know about that. Didn't you say that about that last place we went to? And the one before that? And what? You've eaten at every over-priced Italian restaurant in all of NYC?"

"Practically." He snorted with a little laugh.

She gave him her best look of incredulity.

"What? You know I don't cook. I order a mean takeout though. I can tell you that right now. I love a good Italian restaurant, and this one I'm sure is right up there, and can hold its own amongst the very best in the city."

"Well, when I'm not eating salads, Chinese, or Japanese sushi are probably my favorites. Oh, wait no. Maybe Arabic Shawrma. Or Turkish. They make some incredible, super tasty dishes. Or wait…Thai, now that I think about it. There's nothing to compare with an Asian inspired curry…mmm, now that's the best. Sort of ties all the best of Asian fusion cuisine together. Know what I mean? But still not to be outdone by a good spicy West Indian curry. Trinidad and Jamaica are the best for that, by the way. Such depth of flavor–"

She did a double take as she noticed him watching her. "What?"

"Wow. I've mostly seen you eat salad. You must get taken out to dinner…a lot."

"No, not a lot, unless you mean when I take myself out."

"You do that? Go sit in a restaurant all on your own?"

"Of course I do, on occasion. Don't you?"

"No, not at all. I get a whole lot of fast food, of course, all the time. Takeout mostly. But I definitely don't go on my own to anywhere A-list like this."

"Well, now that's just sad. You're missing out on some serious opportunities for meaningful introspection, my friend."

"Really?" He didn't look convinced.

"Oh, don't look at me like that. Like I'm some pathetic old maid about to expire on a shelf, or something."

"Oh, surely not," he said in a near perfect imitation of her, then grinned.

"Oh, you mock me," she pointed a finger at him, "but I'm telling you; I've been on my own for so long, I can honestly say I've learned how to appreciate my own company. As a matter of fact, sometimes I quite prefer it. As should you, by the way. You know what they say?"

"What's that?"

"Everywhere you go, there you are. The single longest relationship of your life. So, you'd better make nice with yourself, and fast. Because God willing, you'll be together for a very long, healthy and happy time."

"From your lips to God's ears," he clasped his hands together before him as though in prayer. "And I get that, sure. But…uh…don't you ever get lonely though? Doesn't it play on your mind, being on your own so much like that?"

"Sure, sometimes. I'm not going to pretend otherwise. But then I remember the very many awful experiences I had dating Stuart. I've told you about that."

"Ad nauseum. Don't remind me. Even though he's penniless and barely off the street now, I'll still get angry at what he did to you, all over again."

"Right. I know. Sorry. Anyway, so I remember that once I hit my thirties, I got to know myself fairly well. Realized I adore going to the theatre, the opera, eating out at my fave restaurants, spending an obscene amount of money on my trips to the mall. Only sometimes, mind you. Not all the time. But, on shoes…" she reached over and touched his arm as she paused with what she considered to be an appropriate and reverent intake of breath.

"And speaking of which, what is it with you ladies and shoes anyway? I mean, do you seriously need one in every color and style? It's unholy is what it is."

She gasped. "Bite your tongue. Never. *Ever.* Castigate a woman and her shoes. It is absolutely a blessing of God, this pleasure I derive from shoe shopping. Maybe the very best blessing. It's like you men and your silly sporting events, or the way you look at–"

"A beautiful woman." He nodded and gave a low growl.

"I was going to say a sports car. And no. *That*... is lust."

"Not the way I do it."

"Oh, for heaven's sake." She rolled her eyes.

"I'm serious. It's a benediction is what it is. There is no better reminder of God's awesome, unmatched creative genius. Nothing as magnificent, on this side of heaven, as a beautiful and confident woman...dressed to impress..."

"Wait for it..." she leaned in, held up the back of her wrist to his mouth, like she was interviewing him.

"...and wearing six inch 'do-me' heels. Aww yeah..." He winked at her, then barked out a laugh.

"And there it is. The stereotypical male comment. I knew it! Oh, and look at that. We've come full circle, right back to shoes."

"So, we have," he chuckled, "I actually remember lots of trips to the mall with my ex-wife when we were together. She'd stop outside the stores and look at every single shoe display. Sometimes she'd go in and actually buy something, but most of the time she'd stand there and gaze in, and I knew, from past experience she had absolutely no intention of buying. Not even one of 'em. Darndest thing I've ever seen. I remember at first it took me a while to stop bumping into her every time she'd stop, or change direction." He smiled. "It took me a minute to get the shoe window shopping rhythm going. Pretty soon I had all the stops and starts down to a science."

"Okay, so that's likely the single most impressive and noteworthy thing you've told me about yourself so far. How am I only hearing about this hidden talent now?"

"Hey, you never asked. But, now that you know, I'm ready whenever you are. Come on…" he gave her that slow smile of his, accompanied by the sexy gravel in his tone, "take me shoe shopping… I dare yuh."

"Oh, please…" She gave a delicate snort and grinned. "Like you could ever keep up with me."

"Oh, I'll do far more than keep up. I can go for hours. I guarantee it."

"Yes…well, uh…"

She eyed him.

Wondered what was going through his mind just then, given the way he was looking at her.

All humor forgotten, she felt…well…odd…under the weight of that look. But in such a new, exciting, and fun way. His blue gaze was all intriguing and intense. All mystery and captivating focus. Hinting at an extraordinary experience.

And delightful mayhem!

Sensing they were venturing into a conversation that had absolutely nothing to do with shoe shopping, she searched her mind for the thread of her original thought.

"Anyway, where was I? Oh yes, I was telling you about shopping, and then there were a few guided tours of Europe and the Far East that I took. Remember I told you about those? All on my own. Well, except for Holy Spirit as my companion of course. I have to say, I thoroughly enjoyed the solitude. So, shopping, the theater, dining out, traveling," she ticked them each off on a different finger, "do you know what the common denominator driving all of that enjoyment is? I'll give you one guess."

He pointed at her.

"Precisely. Little old me." She lifted, then tipped her glass to him in salute as she wondered about the curious expression he still wore.

He gave her a mysterious little half smile and tipped his own glass in slow response.

"So, thank you so much for inquiring after my mental health, but as you can see, I…am quite fine."

His voice dropped a few octaves to an appreciative, even if contrived, grating rumble.

"Yeah…you sure are."

She did a double take, unable to believe her ears.

"Really? That's twice now, Professor. Three strikes and you're out, my friend." She grinned.

"Crap, where did that come from. I don't even know why I said that." He gave a dry chuckle as he shook his head. "That was beyond lame." She watched as a blush of red crept up from his neck. He took a big swig from the glass he'd just raised to her. "I heard the words coming out and, in my mind, I saw myself like a cartoon character trying to grab them out of the air and jam them back in my mouth, before you could hear me." He gave another dry laugh.

"If only," she smiled. "Not to worry though, I've had that happen more than a few times myself. But still, thank you for the compliment. It's very lovely to hear, however clichéd.

"So, what about you? What do you enjoy doing when you're not teaching?"

"Oh, I'm an avid rock climber. Both Sam and I are. It's one of the ways we've bonded over the years."

"Sounds absolutely wonderful."

"You think? Then you should definitely come with us sometime."

"Who me? Oh, no. That's not happening." She gave an indelicate snort.

He looked both shocked and disappointed at her response.

"Oh, I'm so sorry, that didn't come out right. I meant it's wonderful for you and Sam. Me on the other hand, I can't stand being out in nature with the elements, and the heat, and the bugs and everything. Look in the dictionary under high-maintenance and you're certain to find a pic of me. Smiling. In my Manolo's."

"And look at that, we're back to shoes again." He gave her a quirky smile.

"Oh, my gosh!" She let out a brief laugh. "Okay, so maybe the love affair I have with shoes may border on unnatural, as you say, but teaching? Now that's my real passion. I know it's what I'm meant to do. What about you? Could you ever see yourself doing anything else?"

"Oh, for sure. I wasn't always a teacher. I had a whole other career before this one."

"Is that right? But you're so good at it."

"You think so?"

"Oh, yes. Your students love you. I hear your classes are always some of the first to be filled every semester."

"Well, thanks. It means a lot to get that kind of

validation."

"So, what'd you do before?"

"Tech start-ups mostly. Plus, I was deep into software development that utilizes AI. Well, until I saw just how destructive it was becoming. I helped create some programs that to this day I have no clue how they actually came to be, what they're fully capable of, or what the possible negative implications are.

"I started doing some defense contract work for a particular client. I can't say too much about it, obviously. But suffice it to say they had close ties with the defenders. And everything was going fine until, one night I was working on a particular segment of code. It was for some energy shielding that could absorb the firepower it was taking on and use it to boost itself. Like an inherent power source. I kept hitting a brick wall with the section I was working on, so I stopped for a couple minutes to go get a cup of coffee. You know, to see if I could clear my head, gain some fresh perspective? But when I got back, everything I'd worked on for the past two months was gone. I mean, totally wiped, and in its place was something I can't even describe. A complete rewrite. Different specs and parameters. A totally different deal."

"Wow, so you mean it came up with an entirely new solution for the problem you were trying to solve?"

"No, I mean it completely transformed the original objective I programmed into it. Instead of a defense shield, it created a new weapon. One with a level of destructive power and capability I've never seen. I can't even tell you. It scared me like I've never been scared before. I mean, I was terrified. I remember I didn't sleep a wink that night."

"Oh God, have mercy… What'd you do?"

"I destroyed all the data of course. Did a deep scrub till absolutely no trace of it was left. Cost me a pretty penny to terminate the contract, but I told them I couldn't finish it and cut ties. After that, I started working on my exit plan in a serious way. I'd been feeling for months that I was going through the motions. It stopped being my dream career and started being a serious drain on me and my family, long before then. Don't get me wrong, I was extremely proud of what I'd built, but I was working long hours, neglecting Sam and her mom while she was still in the picture. I'd always enjoyed and felt fulfilled by the training aspect of the job. Like whenever I brought in new people, so something told me teaching would be a good option for me. Never too late to make a change, right?

"Anyway, three months later I sold the business to a rival who'd had his eye on me and my companies for quite a while, and for a very healthy profit. They even wanted to keep me on in a consultative role. But I let them know once I was out, I was out, and started working on my teaching qualifications. Then only two years later I got the opportunity at Sunnyvale, and I haven't looked back since."

"Wow, that's quite a story."

"Yes, and I've never told a soul about what I did until now, so, goes without saying, especially knowing what we do now about the defenders…"

"Say no more. I'll take that secret to my grave.

You can trust me."

"Yeah, I can…" he gave her a strange little look. "So, what about you? What's your story? When did you know teaching was your thing?"

"Probably since I was a teenager. So, coupled with my love for the literary classics. The best job I could ever have is getting to lead a whole new generation to love them the way I do. What can I say, it's a match made in heaven."

"Well, your passion when you teach is evident."

"How would you know?"

"I may or may not have snuck in and sat in the back of one of your classes. After I met you at the store that first day." He grinned.

"Really?"

"You were talking about Othello, and the tragic results that ensue from jealousy and manipulation. I'll never forget it. Your references were powerful, and relatable, and so real. You truly have a gift, you know that? It took me right back to my first infatuation and what happened with us. I've experienced some very destructive jealousy first hand, believe you me. I can relate."

"Oh, is that right? Now you've really got my attention. How so?"

"Well, she was the first girl I ever uh…you know?" He raised his eyebrows.

"Yes, fine. I get the point. What happened?"

"Well, I went a little crazy when I thought she was cheating on me. Confronted her right there in the middle of the school cafeteria."

"The cafeteria?! Exactly how old were you when all this transpired?"

He looked sheepish and adorable at the same time. "Old enough to know better, but not old enough to handle that much physical intimacy. Dang near lost my mind. She was older…more experienced, and I was…uh…let's just say energetic."

His smile held untold mysteries.

Her face felt like it was on fire.

"Right! No need to paint me a picture. Let's move along, shall we?"

"Wait, that's it!"

"What?"

"It has to be thirst, right?"

She gave him a blank look.

"The riddle. Starts with T and ends in dust? Physical thirst can turn to dust if you're not careful."

"Unless you're talking about the kind you can quench with a glass of water. That's not thirst. Haven't we covered this already? That's lust. Again."

"Uh-uh, that's where you're wrong," he shook his head. "Same thing…provided you're doing it right."

This time the gravel in his voice. His half smile. Even the look in his eyes. All were as telling as an open book.

And this time it wasn't only her face that caught his fire.

"But, but…that doesn't even make sense." She dragged her wayward thoughts back to the puzzle they were trying to solve. "How much more eager for the win can we get? We're practically rabid already trying to get out of that infernal maze. I'd say we're well past thirsty."

"Hmmm…I know I am."

He doubled down on his lusty look, and had her face heating up all over again.

"Oh, for heaven's sake, that's three. What is with you tonight? Will you cease and desist please? This is serious."

"Okay, okay." He gave a low growl and shook his head like he was trying to dislodge something. "So, we're plenty thirsty to get out of that hell hole. Point taken. I guess I'm grasping at straws at this stage. Sorry." He ran a hand through his hair.

"No, no…this is good, actually. Keep throwing those ideas out there. No matter how farfetched. We're getting closer. I can feel it. We must be. We merely need to trust each other's instincts on this and we'll…"

And just like a bolt out of the blue, it hit her—

"By Jove…That's it! We have to trust!"

"Huh?"

"I can't believe I didn't figure it out before now. It's so simple, it should have been obvious."

"What are you on about?"

"The answer to the riddle. If to win you dare. This you must. It starts with T. And ends in dust. *Rust* is what ends in dust. Plus, there's the famous idiom 'trust turns to dust', you remember that one, right?"

"Oh, of course. …Grrr…" his growl was deep as he slapped his forehead, "How did we not get that before now. I feel like such an idiot."

"You and me both. We were so busy trying to think of words starting with T that could get dusty eventually, but it's what comes after the T that we should have been focusing on. Rust turns to dust."

"Okay, so to win we must trust…but trust what? I mean, it could be anything. God, each other? Even Gruff."

"Gruff?! Bite your tongue. We're never getting out if I need to trust that mangy, flea-bitten, evil creature."

"Yes. I see how that could be a problem."

"My money's on God. We're literally on a faith journey. This can't be a coincidence. We've both been going to church regularly. We're enrolled in Bible study. This must be the next step. Like a test to see what we've learned and how we apply it… What?"

"I'm not sure about that. He may allow certain things to happen for our own good, but test?" His head tilted to the side.

"Well, maybe not literally, like an exam or something. Although I have seen references to men being tested in the bible. Look at Job. Either way I do think that we need to behave like we remember we're performing for an audience of One."

"Oh, that's good. I like that. Let me guess…Gabriel?"

"Naturally."

"Sweet. I have to remember that one."

"So, what do you think?"

He glanced up, as their server rolled over, trays-for-arms laden with their food.

"I think it's time to eat."

"But–"

"No. No more buts. Relax, God's got this. And whatever it is we need to do, I'll tell you what, once I'm with you, my very own personal, super-secret,

kick-butt ninja. I am good to go."
"Unbelievable…" She rolled her eyes.
He winked at her and grinned.

Chapter 22

Psalms 107:2
Let the redeemed of the LORD say so, whom he hath
redeemed from the hand of the enemy…

"Hey Trudy," Lily called out as she approached her. "Have you seen Jeri in the quad today?" I thought I glimpsed her very early this morning. I swear she's like some kind of ninja, or super-secret spy or something, the way she keeps popping up unannounced."

"Oh yes, I just saw her with Jake. Around five minutes ago. She had him cornered in the faculty rec room."

"What? Are you serious?"

"Yes, I'm pretty sure. It's kinda hard to miss her with those outfits she wears."

"I cannot believe her. She doesn't give up, does she? I mean, what do I have to do? Hang a sign around his neck that says 'hands off, he's mine'?!"

"Well, glad to see yuh got that whole man-claiming thing down pat now, huh?"

"Ooo, that fast, man-stealing, spawn of a

guttersnipe hussy! She's getting on my very last nerve, that one is."

"I can see that. But, yuh might wanna take a beat, and a breath, before you go over there and go off all Montagues vs Capulets on her." Her friend chuckled.

"No, of course not. I'm fine."

"Are you sure? Because you look and sound like a woman in love."

"What? Don't be silly. I'm playing a part. You know? He asked me to guard his six, and that's what I'm doing. That's all. You're being ridiculous, Trudy. Me? In love? I mean the very idea. It's absurd. Laughable really, is what it is."

"Uh-huh…"

Trudy eyed her.

"So, anyway, I better go save the day. Thanks Trudy. I'll catch up with you later?"

"Yeah, sure. You go Supergirl! Go save that man!" Trudy called after her with a laugh as she turned and broke into a sprint to go thwart Jeri's latest brazen act of utter disrespect.

About to march through the open doorway of the breakroom she heard Jake's voice and stopped. Stood where they couldn't see her, right outside, against the wall.

"So, you see, you're great Jeri, I'm sure. But there can't be anything between us. I quite literally love everything about her. Her mind, her beauty, her kindness, her generosity. She's the most unselfish person I've ever met. I love her frankness and her humor, down to those little quirky Shakespearean expressions she uses all the time as though we're in the sixteenth century instead of the twenty-second.

And most of all I love that she's unapologetically herself. She's the real deal. Classy, cultured, and down to earth. She loves God more than anything, or anyone else in the world, and in a time such as ours, where it is wildly unpopular to profess that. Openly. She doesn't give a bad-devil-dang what anyone thinks about her because of her confession of faith. That is phenomenal to me. A woman who knows her mind and is that confident, and completely comfortable in her own skin? It may well be the sexiest thing I've ever seen. So, sorry, but no. This? Whatever you were thinking? It just isn't happening."

"Well, okay then…wow… Well, yuh can't blame a girl for trying, right?" Jeri gave a slight laugh. "Hope she knows how lucky she is. See yuh Jake."

Realizing their conversation was coming to an end, Lily all but leapt over to the nearest doorway, pressed herself into it, and kept her back to the breakroom as she heard Jeri's high heels click against the floor as she exited and headed down the corridor in the opposite direction.

Glancing over her shoulder she saw the coast was clear and turned back. She entered the breakroom where Jake was standing at the food synthesizer. It lit up and a cup of coffee materialized in the dispenser.

"Well, you sure told her."

"Lil!" He spun at the sound of her voice. "Where'd you come from?"

"Heard you were in here with Jeri and thought you might need saving. But clearly, I was mistaken.

That was quite a speech." She walked right up to him.

"Oh, you heard that? Uh…okay…you think so?"

"Oh absolutely, I understand what you did there and I feel exactly the same way."

"You do?" The look of relief on his face was sublime.

"I appreciate you too. So much. Maybe I haven't said it enough, but you're the best friend a girl could have. That I've ever had."

"I know! I…wait…what?"

"Yes. Of course. With everything we've been through, I couldn't have found a better, more solid friend and faith partner to take this journey with me."

"Well, yes…that's true, but listen…about what I said–"

"Oh, not to worry," she waved away his words. "No need to explain. I know you had to put on a little extra over the top for her benefit. To get her off your case. So don't even give it another thought. I'm just glad she finally got the message. You good? It wasn't too unpleasant hurting her feelings like that? I know you've been trying to avoid a scene this entire time. You must be so relieved though, right?"

"Uh…I suppose. But listen–"

"Oh, wait, hold that thought." Her alert to tell her she'd missed her fifteen minutes until class reminder went off. "Oh darn, I've got to run, or I'll be late for class. We'll catch up later, in our usual spot in the sunshine?"

"Yeah…sure."

"Great, you're the best…bestie." She grinned then pulled him down for a quick peck on the cheek. "Don't forget, dinner tomorrow night. Oh, and in case I forget to tell you later, enjoy your day off."

"Oh, right. Thanks." He shook his head like *he'd* forgotten.

"Well?" She paused for a second. "Aren't you going to do that thing we do?"

"What?"

"You know…" She gestured with a hand between them.

"Oh, right. See you around, Lily."

"You wish, Professor."

She smiled.

He nodded, and she turned and hustled to the door.

Chapter 23

John 3:16
For God so loved the world, that he gave his only
begotten Son, that whosoever believeth in him should not
perish, but have everlasting life…

Lily hustled into class in the nick of time.

"Okay people, settle down. We've got a lot to cover today." She placed her notetaker in its customary spot on her desk.

"Now, before we get started on our next lovely literary adventure, I want to share a little something that I think is a very fitting final word about what we've studied so far.

"Sun Tzu, the famous, ancient philosopher said – 'The supreme art of war is to subdue the enemy without fighting.' I think that's brilliant. Don't you? It so perfectly incapsulates the quintessential strategy of the master manipulator."

She walked over to the left side of the space in front of her desk and gestured with a hand.

"First, art…because it reminds us that it absolutely is a craft. So, as you train mind and body through martial arts, the manipulator practices and hones the skill of control through persuasion and intimidation.

"War…" She turned and walked with purpose to the right. Met and held the gazes of several students in the front row, "because make no mistake, the manipulator will engage you in a mental battle. With the aim to dominate, and yes, to subdue. Not in a fight in the traditional sense, but still where the ultimate spoils are your absolute and unequivocal capitulation."

She returned to the center again. Paused, as she prepared to deliver her next line.

"The enemy…because, and perhaps most chilling of all, no matter how you try to convince yourself otherwise, at some point you have to acknowledge that the manipulator, the person who crushed your individuality, to bend you to their will…never, *ever* saw you…as a friend…at all."

Dear God…

Where had that come from? She hadn't even intended to say that. It wasn't part of the notes she'd prepared the night before. She searched her mind for the thread of her original thought. Reached back to her notetaker…

And stopped.

She turned back slowly. Faced her class and allowed that still small voice to guide her instead.

"You know, I won't give you the details, but like so many, I went through my own experience with a master manipulator some time ago. So, while we've been looking at that particular theme all semester through the lens of different literary works, I feel the need to tell you about what it's like to go through and survive a real-life experience. If only in the hope that it will help you avoid it entirely, or at very least mitigate the effects, and yes, the heartbreak. There I said it." She looked around the room and felt heartened by the many answering smiles of encouragement she saw spread out in front of her, across all levels of the classroom.

"It can be insidious. First, it's a critical word here, a negative comment there, and before you know it, you've arrived. At that space where self-doubt festers and thrives. It's not *just* that it robs you of your self-respect. It's not *just* that it makes you question everything you think you know about yourself. It's not *just* that you lose the ability to make even the simplest decision on your own. It's that it's all of that…and so much more.

"I don't want to make a speech because I left my soapbox at home today," she smiled, "and I won't preach to you because…well…one, I'm not qualified, and two, this isn't a religious studies class. But I will say that a deep and abiding faith in God, or even a passing acquaintance, is the beginning of breaking free. Because you quite simply cannot remain trapped in that type of darkness, while you're in the presence of *THE* ultimate light. And because when you're sitting on your bathroom floor, alone, crying your eyes out, and there's no one to turn to but Him? Well, let's just say the truth gets real. Really fast.

"And the truth is…you have to have faith. That though the experience may derail you, it cannot destroy you. That even though you feel like your trust has been trampled, and someone's gone through your chest to your heart with a spoon, you *will* recover. Faith…that yes, oh yes…you will love again.

"I like to think that love goes on. You know? The real love you have for your family, your friends, and that special someone. I feel compelled to share what I've come to believe, and that is that the love of God is beyond anything we could ever begin to fathom, or ever imagine. It stretches across time and space. Across dimensions. Until forever.

"All of that to say, that love, real love, resides in and flows without ceasing from, the presence of the only One who embodies it truly and completely. And it will always be worth the risk. No matter what. So, go ahead, take that leap of faith and dive headfirst into *that* kind of real love. Thumb your nose at fear, secure in the promise of an unimaginable eternity of abiding love, where we no longer measure the intensity of our momentary earthly joy, against the degree of our inevitable despair.

"Choose love…I implore you… Because when you could have had forever, everything else is insignificant, don't you think?"

There was a deafening silence at first, and then the classroom exploded with cheers, applause, and 3-D hearts, flowers, and other electronic affirmations.

"Thanks folks. I appreciate you."

She smiled.

Even as somewhere deep inside herself, she quashed her own lingering personal doubts…

For it was time to stop being afraid.

High time.

Jake knew it was high time he told Lily the truth.

Aside from the benefit of unburdening his soul, it was without a doubt the only way they'd be able to move forward. God knew, he'd tried everything else. He'd run the full gamut. From subtle hints about his feelings, right up to an all-out flirt-fest the last time they'd met for dinner. All while giving her the space to come to him.

Well, he'd had enough. It was time for all-out honesty.

After she'd overheard him talking to Jeri in the faculty kitchen that morning, he'd been ready to come clean. It was only her untimely departure that had stopped him. This time, when they met for dinner, and the topic of his ex-wife came up, as it inevitably did, he'd made up his mind, he wouldn't obfuscate and change the subject. Instead, he'd tell her the whole sordid story about what happened the day Gwen died.

But first he had to tell Sam.

He remembered it like it was yesterday.

The feeling of dread. The horror of feeling totally responsible.

If only he'd tried harder to make their marriage work.

If only he'd stopped her from leaving.

If only he'd taken the time to listen that last time

she'd called him. Gone over to her apartment as she'd asked him to.

If only she hadn't gotten in her car to drive to his house.

If only drunk drivers weren't the leading cause of fatal car accidents.

If only…

Chapter 24

Philippians 2:12
Wherefore, my beloved, as ye have always obeyed, not
as in my presence only, but now much more in my
absence, work out your own salvation with fear and
trembling...

"So, as you can imagine, the number of 'if only' thoughts were endless. I blamed myself for so long. Agonized over every misstep. Plus, I couldn't even tell Sam. Well, not until yesterday. I don't think I can express what it's been like."

"I'm so sorry Jake," she reached across the restaurant table and grasped his hand in support. "I can't even imagine. Carrying the weight of that for so long. All alone. That must have been so awful. I'm so glad you're finally taking steps to make peace with the whole situation."

"I should also say, I wasn't honest with you when you told me about that bad episode you had. You know? When you heard the man's voice telling you not to trust...him. And that you'd wind up like 'her'. I suspect that was about me and Gwen, and I should have said something. Instead, I let you assume it was about Stuart. Can you forgive me?"

"Completely unnecessary," she shook her head. "I sort of put two and two together for myself later on. It was such an obvious and boldfaced attempt by the fallen to sow seeds of doubt and jeopardize the strong trust we were building. I didn't even dignify it with a further thought. I'm so glad you didn't let it drag you back into self-loathing over what happened to her."

"But I did revisit quite a few painful memories. I think more than anything I regretted not bringing her to a place of faith. I tried so many times, and in so many different ways over the years, but I couldn't get her there. In the end I think it's what truly broke us apart. She was going more and more into a lifestyle I couldn't countenance, given where I was in my faith walk, and where I was trying to progress to. And of course, how I wanted to raise Sam."

"Each one of us has to work out our own salvation, with fear and trembling, remember? You can't hold yourself responsible for her walk. That was her choice. I know it's a harsh reality, but that's between her and the Lord. You have to trust that in the end, somehow, in some way, He worked it out for her."

"Yes, but believing that doesn't make it any easier though."

"I know." She squeezed his hand again.

"Anyway, now you know the whole story."

"And thank you for trusting me with it. You were so guarded before. I think we've turned another important corner in our friendship."

"Funny you should say that. I'm glad we have

this time to talk tonight. There's something else I've been meaning to discuss with you."

She looked at her watch.

"Actually…can it wait? I'm so sorry, but I've got some work I have to get done for my first class in the morning. Would you mind terribly if we continued this tomorrow?"

"Oh, right. Yes. Sure. Let's get going."

It appeared as though he wanted to say something else, but he looked down and pulled up the bill on the electronic tab on the table.

She looked around the restaurant as a couple other patrons settled up on their tables, then made their way to the exit.

"Ever wonder what would happen if you tried to dine and dash? I mean, the androids only host and serve. Even though they're on wheels, I would bet that someone could outrun them and get away."

"Well, you could try, but I would strongly advise against it."

"Oh? What's the matter, Jake? Didn't have any bad-boy days? Is that it?" She grinned at him.

"No, I did." His left eyebrow rose as he gave her a quirky smile. "That's actually how I know if you haven't paid, the minute you get to any of the exits of most restaurants, you get a nasty shock."

"Wow, is that right? I had no idea. What kind of shock? Does a holo-security guard jump out of the potted plant near the door, or something?" She burst out laughing.

"No. I mean you get a nasty shock. Literally. From the perimeter forcefield. Enough to put down a horse."

"Okay. Wow." She was stunned. "Good to know. Thanks for that."

"Anytime." He smiled as he shook his head, touched his wrist to the table to pay the tab, and then rose and ushered her out to the street.

"Where's your car? I'll wait with you while you call it around."

"Oh, it's actually in the shop. I took a cab here. I'll call one over," she raised her hand to signal one that was a little way down the street.

"Absolutely not." He grabbed her hand out of the air and held it in his by his side for a moment. "Why didn't you tell me? It's my day off, but I could have come pick you up from the university."

"That's exactly why I didn't tell you. You haven't had a day off in a while. I wanted you to enjoy it. Not have to play chauffeur to me."

"I wouldn't have minded. You know it's right on the way from where I live. And there'll be no cab ride now, by the way. I'll take you home. I insist.

"Ready for pick-up," he spoke into his wrist com.

"That's not necessary, Jake, really. It's late and I don't want to inconvenience you like that. I'll be fine in a cab."

"Oh, rubbish. It's no inconvenience at all. I won't take no for an answer. You live less than a half hour from here. In fact, in the Lambo, I can probably cut it down to fifteen. Look, here it is already."

A car flew up and settled above their heads, casting a deep shadow and vibrating the air around her with the rumble of its powerful engine. Dumbstruck, she followed its progress, as it made a slow descent to the curb…

… Along with her bottom jaw.

It was a brand-spanking-new Lamborghini Star-seeker, in a striking, metallic blue. A near perfect match for the color of his eyes.

Completely stunned in the moment, "Uh… where's the Camri?" was all she could think to say.

"Oh, it's at home."

"So…uh…what's this?"

He smiled. "I told you I had another car, don't you remember?"

"Uh…I…uh…"

She watched his smile widen even as she fumbled for her next words.

"Well, yes. Sure. But when you said you had another car, well, naturally I thought Acura, or Hyundai. Not this. The newest model aerial Lamborghini? This?! This is your weekend car?! How can you even afford something like this?"

"I sold my tech business a few years ago. I think I told you about that."

"Well, yes. I know you said you used to dabble in tech before you started teaching, but clearly you left out a few details. You bought this when you sold your company, you said?"

"Ah… a couple dozen companies…uh… an entire group, actually."

"More than a dozen? So, what? You're some kind of tech billionaire or something?"

"No, of course not. More of a tech millionaire."

"Seriously?" She heard the pitch of her tone climb to barely below a screech with the note of incredulity in it.

"What? You asked." He grinned.

"Wow… Yes. Yes, I did, didn't I?" She turned away.

"Wait." She spun back. "Wait just one minute…that first night we met up in the void, you sat there and listened to me apologize for us winding up together, sitting in Lucifer's Lambo. You didn't say a word, and you knew full well that car was from your imagination and not mine? And you let me think…? Don't you dare laugh, Jake Traynor. This is so not funny. I cannot believe you!" She slapped his arm as he made no attempt to hide his mirth.

"Aww, come on Lil. Do you honestly think with everything going on that would have been an opportune moment for me to announce, "Oh no, it's not you, this is all about me by the way, looks exactly like the one I have parked in my garage," he made a face. "I barely knew you then, remember?"

Well, that was true. He'd have come across as a complete jerk if he'd imparted that bit of info about owning an over fifteen-million-dollar car right off the bat.

"Okay…so I get that. That's actually a fair point."

"Uh-huh… I have to say though, it was so worth it to see the way you reacted. I can't even lie." He erupted again in rich, contagious laughter. "I cannot believe I had the always eloquent and articulate Lily Kavanagh, at a complete loss for words. Now *that* was one for the record books, for real."

"Oh, do shut up, will you?" She slapped his arm again as he roared even louder.

"Let me take you home. You ready?" Still chuckling, he held her hand and helped her climb into his car.

"Okay... You ready?" Jake turned to Lily.

She nodded. *"Lock and load good buddy, let's do this."*

She heard his bark of laughter in her head.

"Really?" He eyed her.

"What? I've always wanted to say that." She grinned.

"That attempt at a full-fledged American accent needs serious work. Plus, we don't even have any weapons. The way you say it, you'd think we have an arsenal, or something. What does that even..." he raised his hands in a gesture of surrender, *"You know what? It's fine. You do you... Let's go."*

Jake stood straight up from his seat in the car, extended his right hand to her. She grasped it and together they walked right through the Lamborghini's dashboard and hood.

Without missing a beat, his other hand shot out.

"Don't even think about it, buddy." He gripped Public Enemy Numero Uno by the throat, as he attempted his customary approach. *"Trust me when I tell you, I am in no mood for your crap tonight. Comprende?"* The lost soul stumbled as he shoved

him back.

"Yeah, good talk. Come on Lil, let's get this over with, shall we?"

He flung the antique door open wide, and they walked through the doorway and out onto the street.

This time, instead of bright sunlight, it was twilight that greeted them.

And something else…

"Aww yeah… Now, that's what I'm talking about." His handsome face set in satisfied, determined lines, Jake nodded towards the curb.

There, in place of their classic carriage this time, was an elaborate leather saddle. Built for two, and it was sitting atop the most magnificent looking creature she'd ever seen.

A full-sized dragon turned its humongous, beautiful blue and golden-green scaly head, and gave them a look out of crystal clear, blue eyes she could only describe as a bold invitation.

Jake started to move towards it and she grasped his arm.

"Are you sure about this?"

"As sure as I've ever been…about anything."

The look in his eyes and on his face told her everything she needed to know.

Well, that…and one more thing…

"Do you trust me?"

He extended his hand to her and every thought of hesitation fled. She grasped it and together they walked side by side to the curb. Their magnificent dragon lowered himself and his mighty wing to a level they could reach. Jake found a foothold, and then another for them, as they climbed with the assistance of the larger scaly protrusions on the animal's long neck and side. Finally, he took a firm hold of the horn of the large saddle, then reached down and pulled her up, he settled her into it, then swung up behind her.

The sensation of the ground falling away as their beautiful beast first rose to its tremendous height and then lifted off was unimaginable. Indescribable excitement and joy flooded her like nothing she'd ever experienced before, as it leapt up and then soared, to tremendous heights. Cutting smoothly through the sky high above the ground with the rhythmic flapping of its mighty wings.

The fresh air around them was sweetly scented, and as she looked ahead, she could just make out the rising of the sun on what was sure to be a beautiful new day.

"Whatever happens…" She heard the deep tone of Jake's voice swirling around her head in a brand-new way. *"I'm so glad we're together. I couldn't have done any of this without you. You know that, right?"*

She glanced back as he squeezed her waist.

"Yes… I do because I feel exactly the same way. This place is horrific and chaotic but the entire experience has been so cathartic. And I know I owe a lot of that to you. I used to be so spooked by the lost souls and the fallen. Especially when I could sense them and knew they were there, but couldn't see them because they stayed invisible. Having you by my side made it all bearable. And now, well now it's like I can handle anything, by God's grace. Whenever I feel them, agitating. Raging all around me. I have

this peace that allows me to stay calm in the midst of the storm.”

“Oh my God, Lil. That’s it. That’s your gift.”

“What?”

“The gift you told me about? You said you didn’t think you had a gift of Holy Spirit. But you do. Discerning spirits is your gift. Think about it. How many times have you seen them long before I did? Felt their presence the way you described, but couldn’t see them?”

“Oh, wow. You know I think you may be right. I always thought the gifts were earth-bound. It never occurred to me that mine would only manifest in this realm.”

“Well, it’s certainly served you well. It’s served us well. Saved us more times than I can count. I for one am very grateful.”

“So am I, and for much more than that. I know we’ve been battling the fallen in here and in the real world. The stand-off of all stand-offs. For our eternal souls. But in some ways, I feel as though I’ve had a personal reckoning too. I’m finally free of all my emotional baggage. You know, I left California to close that chapter of my life, but what I didn’t realize until recently is that I brought along every little bit of the bitterness and hurt with me. The lack of trust, and fear, and self-loathing that caused me to want to leave in the first place. Well, I’ve renewed my trust and faith in God, stared terror in the face multiple times now, and in a host of ways, and bless God, instead of fear, I feel I now also have the spirit of His power, and such love.”

“Amen to that. I know what you mean. I was

carrying around the weight of guilt over Gwen for so long. I just couldn't forgive myself. It's taken me this long to realize there's nothing to forgive. I didn't trust anyone or even myself enough to deal with the toll it was taking. Being able to fully trust God again, and you, enough to unburden myself has meant more to me than I could ever express. I feel like a new man."

"And I can finally turn to a new chapter in my life. So, thank you, Jake, for taking this journey with me. I couldn't have asked for a better companion."

"Well, looks to me like you both benefitted a great deal from this whole experience."

A voice she hadn't heard in quite a while echoed around her head.

"Did you...?" Both she and Jake said at the same time. She looked back over her shoulder and met his perplexed gaze and blurry expression.

"Was that Uri?"

SNAP!

Feeling like her heart was about to explode in her chest Lily gasped for breath as suddenly without ceremony or warning, they dropped a couple hundred feet in a nano second and were once again standing on solid ground.

Kind of.

She wobbled a bit, extended her arms, then got her bearings. They were in the middle of the desert, right near the entrance to their beautiful oasis by the looks of it. Right back where they started, and witnessing a transformation such as she could never ever have imagined – as their magnificent dragon, with wings flapping in the air, gradually transformed into an even more amazing angel she knew and loved.

In sheer wonder, she watched as the extraordinary, large scaly head was replaced by his handsome and familiar countenance. Massive scaly chest and back, and powerful legs changed. Last of all were his magnificent wings that maintained their enormous span, but changed into lushly feathered luminous white, for a mere second before they disappeared altogether. Completely and extraordinarily altered, he morphed back into him, in a truly awe-inspiring display. All except for his stunning blue eyes of course, that continued to shine ever so bright. Reaching out to her with their customary God given holy fire of all-encompassing wisdom, love, and compassion. Looking like a 21st century movie star, with golden hair blowing around his head, he made a slow descent and landed with enviable angelic power and grace, right beside them.

"Now that…that was *more* than worth the price of admission. Am I right, Jake?" She resisted the urge to giggle like an ingénue, and beamed instead as she glanced over at him.

"Great. Terrific. Best thing I've ever seen," he said from where he stood bent over with his hands resting on his knees. "Seriously, Uri? Is this finally over? And will you please stop doing that 'snap us practically into oblivion' thing? I keep telling you, man. I'm not as young as I used to be."

She chuckled, as his cheeks stretched out on a breath.

After all this time, he still looked like he was about to hurl.

She shared a grin with Uri as he reached out and gave him a single firm pat on the back.

"How's that? Better?"

"Wait… How'd you do that?" His back straightened in an instant, and he went from looking ill to stunned. "That was amazing. I haven't felt this great in years."

"Touched by an angel." She smiled.

"Cliché, but yes, so on the nose."

"Glad I could help." Uri smiled.

"So, hang on… you mean to tell me you could have done that before to make me feel better? All those times you snapped us, and I thought I was about to pass out? Why am I only getting the benefit of this talent of yours now?"

"Hey, this kind of 'Three in One feel good' gift isn't meant for folks on your side of heaven. It can be addictive. Trust me. I did you a favor."

Jake started to say something, then paused. A look of serenity and pure joy crossed his features.

"Okay, you may have a point."

"Uh-huh…" Uri nodded.

"So, all of this… this entire void experience was all your doing?" She turned to Uri.

"Well, no. Not all of it. I built in some stuff, sure. You know? Some options when you needed them. Like the code on the cloth, and some safeguards of course after your first bad experience with Jake's freaky, turban-wearing, what'd you call him? Gruff the starving dragon. Now that was a good one." He held out his fist and barked out a laugh.

"Yeah, it was." She giggled as she bumped it with hers, while Jake stood by with a vague look of disgust on his face.

"I thought your D.I.E.T. experiences were all oases in the desert and dream vacations."

"Not always. Sometimes they're adrenalin pumping wake up calls, but always exactly what you need, when you need it, to get you back on course."

"But the truck though. Come on man, was that really necessary?" Jake's expression suggested he was reliving every single painful memory.

"Hey, you did that to you. I know you realized how the atmosphere started to change whenever you two got angry and started bickering."

"Well yes, but–"

"But nothing. You weren't behaving like grown-ups then. The fact that you handled your situation with kindness, and mutual respect, and trust tonight means you could have done that months ago. And whose fault is that?"

He glanced back and forth between them and didn't wait for a response.

"Exactly. Besides, you were never in any real danger. You've been given a real gift. Both of you. You've actually seen firsthand how God works with you through the very worst experiences of your life. That no matter how bad things seem, you can trust He will always make them work for your ultimate good."

"So, what now?" Jake wondered.

"Now you go home. Just look up and head into the light. Lil? You know what to do, right?"

She nodded.

"Well Professors, I'd say you've learned everything you needed to. As for the rest, well that's all up to you now. Until we meet again. Stay blessed you two."

He disappeared with a smile.

"Uri? Wait!" Jake called after his disappearing form. Then, just as fast as they'd landed in the desert they were back in the dull blurry darkness of the void.

"So, what? He couldn't give us a ride to the light? I'd even take the snapping fingers thing if it meant we would have been back in our beds. What are we supposed to do now?" He looked around at the surrounding darkness and then down. *"Unbelievable…"* He lifted one bare foot and then the other. *"Ever wonder why we don't ever have shoes on in this place. I mean we're always dressed in regular clothes, so why the bare feet? It doesn't make any sense."*

"Oh, I don't know about that. I think it makes perfect sense."

"Oh? Why's that?"

"Because… who needs shoes, when your feet never have to touch the ground."

She grasped his hand and grinned.

"Wha–?"

His aborted question turned into an excited shout as she gathered her power, and launched them high up into the air. Then kept on going. Flying fast, she held his hand in a tight grasp as she arced through the dark night sky heading for the distant light.

"Oh Wow! Lil? This is so amazing! You can fly?"

She nodded with a smile as she slowed their pace and tugged on his hand to pull him forward so he could float alongside her.

"I had no idea. Since when?"

"Since ever."

"And why am I only learning about this now?"

"You never asked Professor."

"Oh, right. Because of course the burning question in my mind when I saw you in the void that first time was, "Say, can you make like a superhero and fly us out of this mess?" He smiled.

"Well, now that you mention it, that would have been kind of unlikely."

"Oh, you think?" His smile turned into a grin.

"Also, it's strange, but I couldn't before when I was with you, until now. It was almost as if I..."

She considered whether she should share her thoughts.

"Almost as if what? Go on... you can tell me."

"Okay... I think...and huge disclaimer by the way, this is only a theory. I think we had to get to this point, where we trusted each other as we are. As the riddle said. Enough to work together as we have for months. It was never about us having to be alike, and trying to think exactly the same because we can't. We're two different people and that's the beauty of it. That's precisely what works. It's about learning to trust because even when you don't know what's next. You know who you're with.

"I feel as though I'm seeing you through a fresh new lens now. Not my cloudy, distorted, weighed down by ex-boyfriend baggage and negative perceptions of men in general that I learned from my relationship with Stuart. I see you. Just you. And I feel... so comfortable, I guess is the best way to

describe it."

"Truly? Is that real, or the adrenalin high from all we've gone through tonight that's talking right now?"

"Oh, it's real all right. I don't know how else to explain it other than to say I feel safe being me...with you. Whether we're here, or back in the world for that matter. The me who I don't let anyone else see. The me who can be quite silly and sometimes annoying. The me who's insecure and fragile and sometimes incredibly temperamental for no good reason. And with the deepest gratitude, that again includes the me who remembers she has the power to fly like the wind through this crazy place."

They shared a smile.

"And I feel as though this whole experience was a spectacular metaphor for who you are to me. All that you are. You are such a fascinating, delightful, surprising, and wondrous puzzle, Lily Kavanagh." His voice in her mind dropped to a soft rumble.

She slowed, then stopped. Turned towards him as they hung suspended in mid-air, face to face.

"Really? You think so?"

"Oh, without even the tiniest sliver of doubt, and in all the best possible ways."

He gave a little tug on their joined hands. Attempted to pull her in closer.

She drifted forward a bit, sensing what he wanted. But not sure if she wanted it too; she pulled away instead. Turned to look in the opposite direction.

She'd wanted to express her sincere gratitude and appreciation for the depth of their friendship, of course…but not incite a passion in him for more than that.

"Come on, we should go." She opted to return the tug on his hand in place of meeting him in a place of such vulnerability. *"We don't want to lose the light,"* she pointed to the glow on the horizon.

"Oh…yes, uh…sure. Let's go home."

She gathered her power about her, and propelled them forward. Used it to distract herself from the sad tone of his voice continuing to echo around her brain, along with worst kind of silence. That of her own making.

And in the answering emptiness in her solitary heart.

Chapter 25

1 Corinthians 13:10
But when that which is perfect is come, then that
which is in part shall be done away...

Lily's heart was officially full to bursting.

Rivalled perhaps only by her full tummy at that very moment.

"Oh, I am stuffed. I definitely should not have had that pasta and the seven-layer chocolate cake, too," she groaned.

"Yes, you absolutely should have. Can't believe I got you to order the same thing I had tonight. This is another one for the record books for sure. Two days in a row. What's happening right now?" He started to chuckle and dodged her attempt to also repeat her slap to his arm.

"Come on now, you know you enjoyed it. It was amazing, wasn't it?"

"Fantastic. And I'll be paying for it when I have to spend an extra half hour every day next week exercising, thank you very much."

"What for? You look amazing Lil. In all the right places…"

"Uh-huh… Watch it, Professor." She felt her face heat at the blatant appreciation in his gaze as it ran over her.

"I thought I was watching… You didn't notice? Dang… I must not be doing it right then." He barked out a laugh.

"Ha-Ha, funny man. Seriously though, dinner was wonderful, as usual. Thank you so much, Jake, and for this especially." She let out a muffled shriek and did a little dance on the spot as she hugged her newest prized possession. "I still can't believe I am now the proud owner of an actual honest to goodness, paper, bound with leather and glue, hardcover book." She beamed as she cradled her very own printed copy of *To Kill a Mockingbird* that he'd presented to her as a gift before they'd sat down to dinner.

"I'm truly quite literally in shock. I mean…aside from the cost, books like this are incredibly rare and difficult to find. How did you even source a copy?" She tucked it safely into her handbag.

"A whole lot of googling. And you can thank Sam for most of that."

"Wow, well thank you again. Ever so much. I will cherish it, always. And thank Sam for me too."

"You are most welcome, from both of us." He smiled.

"By the way, where is Sam tonight? I missed her."

"Oh, she ditched us. A group of her friends are camping outside Madison Square Garden overnight to get in line for tickets for some new high tech music event next week."

"And would those *friends* include the boyfriend?"

"Yes. Dauntless came over last night and asked for permission to take her."

"And you're letting her go?"

"Yes, of course. She's eighteen. Plus, it's going to be this whole big thing. Like a street party since so many people are joining the overnight queue. There'll be music and food. There'll also be a couple private security firms patrolling, hired by the promoters of the event and everything. I… What? Why are you looking at me like that?"

She closed her mouth. "I think I'm in shock. Look at you! Where's the over-protective smothering dad I met in a grocery store and grew to know and love, huh? What'd you do with him?" She barked out a laugh.

"Ha-Ha. Very funny."

"I'm serious. This is quite a transformation. Good for you. Real progress. Sam must be thrilled."

"Oh, she is. She told me to thank you for her."

"Oh, rubbish! I did nothing. This is all you."

"It is most certainly not rubbish. If it wasn't for you, I'd still be trying to control her every move. Alienating her in the process, instead of trusting in her ability to mirror the Godly values I spent her entire childhood instilling in her. That is all due to your influence and guidance, and I can't thank you enough for it."

"Well, you are most welcome. I'm so glad I could help. You two are my family now." She put a hand on his chest, reached up on her tiptoes, pressed her lips in a soft kiss to his cheek. Met his gaze, and got lost in its intensity all at once.

And completely forgot her customary retreat…

Time stood still…as he ran the pad of his thumb across her lower lip.

Once.

And once again…

"Yuh know…you still owe me that one kiss…"

He shifted his hand. Ran his knuckles in a slight caress against her jawline. Then warm palms down her bare arms from her shoulders, compelling their continued eye contact. Kept the distance between their faces just the same. Followed her… As she slowly lowered the heels of her shoes to the ground.

Even then, he kept on coming. She held her breath. Felt his. Nearly imperceptible, brush her cheek. Watched his face…getting ever closer and closer to hers…

"But…Jeri's nowhere around though. Remember the rules?" Her voice came out breathy. "Plus, it's getting kinda late. I should go," she mumbled as she took her hand off his chest. Ducked her head a bit. Looked to her right at the oncoming traffic on the street in front of the restaurant then looked back up at him. Took in his expression that went from perplexed… to disappointed…and then a little sad?

"Okay, so that was beyond embarrassing." He let go of her upper arms and took a step back.

"Oh, fiddlesticks. I'm so sorry. That was entirely my fault. I don't know what got into me. I shouldn't have uh…engaged with you like that."

"Engaged with me? What? Are you even listening to yourself? I tried to kiss you, Lil, and you make it sound as though you have to fend off a skirmish?"

"Look, it's like this, I don't think this," she gestured between the two of them, "is a good idea. Uh…you and me getting that close. Being more… than we are, I mean."

And then it dawned on her…

"Wait. Is that why you waited till last night to tell me about your financial situation? And show me the car, and now the book, and everything? What? Was this all part of your plan? Did you think I would fall into your arms like some kind of gold digger–?"

"No. In fact. Hell no. That is categorically not what any of this is about. I have feelings for you, Lil. Strong feelings. As I thought you have for me, and that I'd very much like for us to explore. I just didn't want any secrets between us when we took it further. I wanted you to be comfortable that you're getting all of me. As I know everything about you. Or, at least I thought I did."

"And yes, I appreciate that so much Jake. I really do. And look, if it makes you feel any better it's not about you, it's me. I–"

"Stop! Please. Don't say anything more. Unbelievable. You did not just use the 'it's not you, it's me' line on me right now. Like some 21st century, every other rom-com loser guy to some needy chick scenario. I cannot believe this." He ran agitated hands through his hair as he paced away from her a few steps, then came back as she tried to explain.

"I know how it sounds, believe me, but I promise you it's true. You are amazing and any woman would be so blessed to have you."

"Ha! Right. Any woman except you, you mean."

"Look, I don't know what else to say, except it's personal. And because we've become such good friends. So much so, I feel I can share with you what I think, that ultimately, I'd be more comfortable with someone who's more...uh... how do I say this...? Without sounding insensitive. More like... uh...me. I guess."

She shrugged and at first, he looked confused, until his eyes widened.

"Wow..." he ran a hand through his hair again and gave a dry laugh. "I've read about the racist and gender prejudice that existed before the defenders came. I was a child then, so I never experienced it. And now...facing it here, in this moment, I have to say... It stings."

"Don't be ridiculous Jake, this isn't prejudice. This is about preference. I love you as a friend. My very best friend in the world. Come on now... You know that. But as for a boyfriend? Well...in my man... I'd simply prefer–"

"Seriously? Are you even listening to yourself right now? You sound exactly like them. The, oh, I'm not racist. See? I have a whole bunch of, insert your choice of whatever type of person you've convinced yourself you see as equal, when you really don't, friends. What every pseudo race conscious person from the abolition of slavery to the end of the 21st century told themselves to feel better about their societal, institutional, and administration-instilled, intrinsic bias against people who didn't look like them."

"Oh, so you're lecturing me now, Professor? Is that what's happening?"

"No, not at all. But certainly, for the sake of our friendship, I think this is worth ventilating. Don't you? So, come on. Talk to me." He moved in closer. Crossed his arms. Crowded her. So close, she had to crane her neck to look up into his face as he towered over her. "You're saying you'd prefer someone, oh, I don't know, like maybe Stuart? The winner you were with back in Cali last year? A relationship so bad you had to move clear across the country to get some peace of mind and closure? The one who hit you."

She felt every muscle in her body flinch at the harshness of that statement, but still he carried on unabated.

"The one who couldn't respect your beliefs, or the collaborative, loving, and concerted exercise in restraint they require. The one who couldn't keep it in his pants. That guy? Who cheated on you every chance he got. AND then, had the ultimate, unmitigated temerity to blame you for his disloyalty? You mean a great *man-child* like that? That's what you want?"

She resisted the urge to cringe at such a stark reminder coming from someone she'd trusted with one of her deepest held, and most painful episodes of secret shame.

"Now, wait just one minute." Her voice came out soft. Steady. "That's not fair and you know it. I told you those things about my life, in confidence, deeply personal things about my misjudgment, and certainly not to have you fling them back at me when you think it'll score you some brownie points by comparison. Besides, all men cheat, regardless of race or whatever."

"No. They do not." He enunciated every word with a clarity the English teacher in her found laudable.

He shook his head. "I… Don't." His usually full, attractive lips compressed into a tight line. "Plus, I would never manipulate you or try to control you the way he did. I have way too much respect for women, and for you in particular, to ever do that. And…*you* know that."

She did. And she believed every word he said. Knew it was the God's honest truth. Unequivocally. With every fiber of her being, and because of the man she knew him to be. The powerful man of God she'd been fortunate enough to befriend. He'd never cheat on a woman or disrespect her. No matter what. Not ever.

They stared at each other for long moments.

He blew out a breath, took a step back, and then another. Closed his eyes and rocked his head to the left and then the right. Rolled his head. Rested his chin on his chest. All the while she watched as he physically relaxed. Knowing him as she did, she witnessed the change in him as he let the tension ease out of every muscle in his neck and broad shoulders. He rubbed a hand along his chin.

"Okay, look I'm sorry, you were absolutely right." He held up his palms as he shook his head. His voice low and measured. "I shouldn't have said what I did. About your ex. I shouldn't have broken our trust like that. I want you to know you can come to me anytime. Tell me anything and not worry that I'll weaponize it later. I never want to do anything to jeopardize our friendship. It means far too much to me. So, if that's all you want for us." He shrugged. "I respect that and I'm here for it. All day long. Whatever you want." His warm blue gaze met hers. "Can you forgive me?"

"Of course, Jake. Of course. And I'm so sorry if I hurt your feelings. You have to know that wasn't my intention. Our friendship means absolutely everything to me too." She moved to close the gap between them. Both the emotional one she'd created with her words, and the physical one he'd opened up by stepping away from her. She stepped forward, reached up, pulled him in even closer as she put her arms around his broad shoulders. Rubbed his back, then caressed the base of his neck as she tucked him into her warmest and most secure embrace. "You know I love you, right? So much." She leaned back a bit. Looked up into his eyes, to reassure herself that all was well with them, and in their world again. And got caught instead.

Again.

In the sheer intensity that was him. The depth of heat, intriguing intent, and love, reflected back at her in the oasis of his gaze.

His eyelids got hooded as his eyes trapped her in a haven of deep crystal blue. Her gaze shifted. She watched his mouth part on a breath. Or maybe he was about to say something. Either way, before she could think better of it, she slid her hand up from his neck, felt the velvet soft yet spiky comfort of his hair as she ran her fingers through, then grasped the back of his head.

And then pulled him…and his lips…on a slow, inexorable journey to hers.

Watched as his eyes searched hers…darting left, then right. And for the longest second, before she let hers close, and her lips…part…

To welcome a kiss beyond her wildest imaginings.

Fulfilling. Powerful. Excuse-shattering, and life altering.

Sweet and light, then deep, hot, and intense, their mouths met again and again, then clung. He wrested control from her with hungry intent as he delved even deeper, and she willingly relinquished it, to follow his lead. A willing participant, in the ensuing, breath-robbing, sweet, hot tangle of mouths and hearts.

And then when they finally broke apart–

"By Jove…" was all she could manage.

She felt stunned. Searched his face, for a clue to what happened. Giddy, she wobbled a bit, even as she held onto his muscled forearms.

"By Jove, indeed." His voice was a grating rumble as he helped steady her, and as his lips parted on a slow smile.

His head tilted ever so slightly to the side in a breathtaking, familiar pose. "So…I guess this means I'll definitely be seeing you around then, Lily."

"Oh…most definitely…in fact, I think your wish…is now my command, Professor," she breathed.

His eyes darted back and forth as they searched hers.

Again.

"Really?"

His gaze – intense. As he continued to hold her upright and inches away for a second more.

Then two.

Before pulling her back in. Not waiting for her response, or permission to take control this time, as he grasped the nape of her neck and took her mouth with breath stealing and insatiable hunger.

Almost overwhelmed by the potent expression of his desire at first, she soon caught his fire. Energized, she met the undeniable tug and pull, every lick and nibble he offered.

She took… Everything he so willingly gave her, and gave it right back.

Really.

Chapter 26

1 John 4:18
There is no fear in love; but perfect love casteth out
fear: because fear hath torment. He that feareth is not
made perfect in love…

"Really…?"

She jumped at the sound of the voice behind her.
Ye gads! Jake…

"I know you got every single one of my calls,
texts, and messages last night. I even sent out one of
those dang electronic love pigeon-drone things. So,
I'm not even going to ask about that. And now today,
you've obviously been hiding from me all day. Come
on… Lil?"

She cringed.

"Will you please be a grown-up and turn
around? It's not like if you don't look at me, I'll go
away. I'm standing right here after all."

Well duh… she was tempted to be juvenile and
say, but instead she looked up as he took the initiative
and stepped around to stand in front of her. Met his
luminous, stunning, blue gaze.

How could it be that something she'd barely

noticed about him before was now all she could see? Limitless. Was the word that came to mind. Pulling her into his very soul with every blink and wondrous reopening of his awe-inspiring eyes, that were quite simply…captivating.

"What happened since we kissed last night? Don't tell me you changed your mind about us already. Look, I know you were probably surprised." He looked around and lowered his voice as a lone student rushed out of a nearby classroom and headed for the exit. "God knows, it shocked the heck outta me, and I've been praying for us to get together like that. For months now. I even talked to Uri to get his advice. And Gabriel."

"What?!"

The student glanced back as she got to the door.

"You brought Uri *and* Gabriel into this?" She dropped her own voice to just above a whisper, even though they were once again alone with the closing of the external doors behind the student.

"Well yes, I figured Uri knows us very well, and our situation, so I asked for his help. I only spoke to Gabriel that one time, right after the two of us spoke with him together at the rally. It was strange, he got me to open up about my feelings for you, even though I'm pretty sure I didn't want to. But I'll tell you what, I'm glad I did because everything they both told me was spot on."

"I don't even want to know." She sighed and shook her head, thinking she'd melt from embarrassment right there on the spot.

"Maybe not, but you do know we need to talk about this…that kiss…last night. I mean… Wow.

And what you said about us. You blew my mind, Lil… So, we need to talk about it, sometime, right?"

As he said, she'd managed to successfully avoid him all day. Afraid to face what they'd started, before she'd run away like a coward. What she'd felt the night before and all that day, despite her best efforts to suppress and deny it. Deny herself and the simple inescapable truth that she was completely, utterly, and gloriously in love.

With him.

And after everything she'd so stupidly said the night before, she'd be hog-tied to a mule if she'd ever let him know it.

Just her luck that her problem student would choose today of all days to delay her after her last session. She'd finally been able to end their conversation with a promise to think about a course of action that best addressed his articulated difficulty with her class. Intending to make a run for it, she'd almost made it down the hallway too. She hadn't even heard him, until he came up right behind her.

Looking past him, she could see the nearly deserted teachers' carpark right through the laser reinforced glass doors a few dozen meters away, and right down the hall. Beyond his gorgeous face, broad shoulders, muscled arms, trim abdomen, long legs…

By Jove…

There she went again. She'd never have thought all that about him before last night. Now, suddenly she was hyper-aware of every aspect of him and his irresistible anatomy, in a whole new yet still so familiar manner. Disturbing. To be sure. But still in such an enticing way.

She took in a deep breath.

Tried to still the nerve endings all over her body that were suddenly buzzing. Clamoring for her attention like never before. Clamoring for him. All because he was right there. Near enough to touch, to hold...

"No-ooo," she gritted out, partly to him, but mostly to herself. "No." She shook her head for good measure, and with such vigor several long wavy strands of her hair came loose from her makeshift bun so she had to brush them off her cheeks. "We actually don't need to talk about anything. That's the beauty of the spoken word. My favorite aspect of it, if you ask me. That sometimes when you don't want to speak you can simply shut the heck up. Okay?"

She spared him a quick look. Not sure she could handle his reaction, she made ready to walk right past him, coward that she was. Bolt and not look back, as she'd done the night before.

Thought her little speech had worked well enough to put him off too.

Well, at least until he grabbed her arm.

She heard his low growl even as he spun them both around. Marched her down the hall, across the corridor, waved open a door, and then firmly but still somehow gently pushed her into the small room beyond it, and that she didn't think she'd ever noticed was there before.

It was dim. Maybe six by six square. And it smelt like pine disinfectant and...a mixture of both old and new paper? She'd only been around actual paper a few times, and for a very brief period of time. Well...until the night before. Despite her best attempts, she'd been unable to purchase any of the coveted printed versions of the classic books she cherished. Which is why the copy of *To Kill a Mockingbird* that he'd given her the night before was so extra special.

The lighting fixture overhead obviously needed to be replaced, as every now and again it lit the space, for a second. And only enough for her to see its interior, barely. Straight ahead was a bare wall. To the right, as she'd suspected, a couple of old books, a small stack of notebooks, some loose sheets of paper, and other stationery, and electronic notetakers graced some shelving, and on the left, a small garbage bin and a mop and bucket.

And at her back…

Him.

She could sense him, standing right behind her. So close, she felt the heat of his big body. Even his grating breaths on the back of her neck she fancied, but maybe that was her overactive, secret, romance novel-loving imagination.

She took her time turning. Pressed her back against the wall as she faced him.

He took a step forward, completely eradicating the little distance she'd managed to create by retreating to the wall.

She took in a slow breath and looked up. Mesmerized by the captivating flashes of him revealed to her in eye-catching intervals by the flickering light.

"Okay, Professor. So…you want to tell me why I'm standing in a supply closet right now?" Her voice came out sounding a whole lot steadier than she felt right then. Score one for her.

"With me, you mean?"

He smiled, brushed a couple remaining strands of her hair off her cheek and her lips. Tucked them behind her ear. His touch sending shock waves through her, and her nerve endings from buzzing, directly to full-on screaming awareness.

"Uh… Sorry?" She fought to focus on what he'd just said amid the thrumming in her body. "Uh, yes, of course with you. True the lighting's pretty bad, but I don't see anyone else in here. Do you?"

He gave a low chuckle.

"Okay, so…" He cleared his throat, but his voice still came out deep and husky. "So, look. I had every intention of us talking this out, once we got in here. Believe me. But now…" He gazed down at her. Lost his smile.

"But now…?" she breathed.

He moved in even closer, till she could feel his thighs, lightly touching hers. Watched his head slowly descend in the flickering light. Inch by agonizing inch. A master of the art…compelling her complete surrender. Wresting away from her every single denial she'd thought she should raise right then.

And to his credit, all without ever uttering a single word.

"Oh, dash it… not again," she whispered, as she relented, grasped his forearms, and tiptoed up to meet him.

Then just held on.

This time he controlled their pace from the start. Took his time. Let her play with the taste of him as he devoured her mouth by slow degrees. Until she could not summon the will to protest. To do anything but let him kiss her, as she kissed him right back.

"Okay, yes," she breathed against his lips then nodded when he at last let them come up for air.

"Yes?" His look was a mixture of mild surprise and amusement.

"Yes. My answer is yes," she affirmed.

"Yes, to what Lil? I haven't even asked you anything yet." His smile was sexy-good. He reached down again. Alternately licked then nibbled on her lips for long mind-numbing seconds.

"Uh, you haven't?" She looked up once he was done, met his amused gaze.

"No, I haven't."

"Oh, okay. Really? Could have sworn there was a question in there somewhere."

"No…" He dragged his half open mouth along her cheek down to her neck and back up again.

"But still, the answer's yes." She grasped his neck. Urged his gaze to hers in the flickering light. "I love you, more than I've ever loved any man. When I'm with you I feel safe and cherished. You look at me with those gorgeous blue eyes and it's like I'm the only one in the room. I feel beautiful, and special…and seen. And incredibly you're my best friend in faith and in the world. How could I ever be so blessed." Still amazed, she shook her head with a smile. "I thought I'd conquered my fear. I knew I was ready to love again. But I wasn't prepared for the sheer depth of my feelings for you. I got scared again last night. But I'm not anymore. I'm a new woman, thanks to you, and I very much wanted you to know that." She took in a shaky breath.

"Do you realize…this is the first time you've made it through an entire conversation like that, without ever mentioning what's-his-face?"

"Who?" She tilted her head to the side…gave him her very best half smile.

"That's my girl…" He returned her smile. "Such a good answer…"

"It's all because of you, Jake. *You*…did that. You're my person. You get me. You're the reason I'm ready… Ready to give you my all now. Everything I am. Everything I ever will be… I'm yours, Jake."

"Mine…" He let out a low and primal growl. His smile was slow, intriguing, and did things to her she couldn't begin to describe. Crazy-good things. "Oh yes… I think I like the sound of that…a lot." He took her lips in a long, voracious kiss.

"So, yes…yes to us."

"*Us*… Now that I love even better." He brushed a thumb across her cheek, smiled, and kissed her again. "And I meant what I said that day. You know? That day you heard me talking to Jeri in the breakroom? Plus, what I think you *didn't* hear. Which is what I told her at the start. That I'm completely. Hope—*fully*," he smiled, "incredibly, and utterly in love…with you. You're my heart… My everything. I didn't tell you at the time, but I meant every word, and not as a friend.

"I love everything about you Lil. Your deep and abiding faith. The way that beautiful mind works. The way you say things like fiddlesticks, and by Jove, and lackwit. I think I've loved you ever since we met up in that grocery store. There you were, my very own exquisite, incomparable, precious little Lily." He smiled and nodded, then took her lips again in a deep and drugging kiss.

"Wait…" she grabbed his neck again, felt her back hit the wall as she pulled away from him a fraction. "What about Sam? What does she think about all this?"

"Oh, she's thrilled. When I told her what happened last night, she kept asking me when exactly was I planning on telling you I loved you, and why I'd taken this long to kiss you."

"Oh, okay. Well, that's so good to know."

"She said she can't wait till I make you my kickie-wifey, I think she said."

"What?" She giggled. "Oh, you mean kickie-wickie. A-plus for effort though."

"Mm-hmm." He put his hands up to her hair and she felt a gentle tug and then the fall of it down to her shoulders, as he pulled out the single clip keeping it in place.

"What are you doing?"

"Testing a theory."

"Wha–?"

"Shh…" He pulled her back into him, caressed its length, and then plunged his fingers in right to her scalp. He inhaled deep.

Smiled…

Right before he pressed a series of soft, sucking kisses to her lips, all while he said, "Now…unlike all the classrooms…this room isn't soundproof…but it is fitted to vacuum seal after hours…once the door is closed…to preserve the precious paper stock in here…"

"Seriously…? How would you even know all that?" She pulled away as she struggled to follow the significance of what he was saying amid the more than pleasant, utterly distracting sensation of his lips and his fingers caressing her hair at the base of her neck.

"Thanks to Duncan, the NYPD detective I told you about, I was fascinated by paper and old writing instruments for a while, so I did a stint of stationery duty. Not important. What is important is I figure we've only got about five minutes of air left in here, then we'll need to get out. So, Lil…?"

"Professor?"

"Shut up, please, so I can kiss you like I want to."

"Uh-huh."

And she let him…

EPILOGUE

"Melanie…" he ran a hand through the thick, lush, black waves of his hair, "don't take this the wrong way, but for pity's sake, will you shut up for one second so I can think…please?"

His voice was mild but he wasn't fooling her for one second.

She knew better. She knew him. There was absolutely nothing mild about Trenton Dorchester, III. Because beneath that calm exterior and tone lay fire. And she knew exactly how to stoke it.

He wanted to play games? Well so be it. He'd met his match in her this time. She was more than up for the challenge. He was about to be in for the mother of all battles.

"No, Mr. Dorchester. I will not shut up! I cannot believe you. I mean…what the heck is this?!" She looked over the side of the sleek, silver flying ship for at least the fifth time in probably as many minutes, hoping against hope that her lofty and jaw-dropping view of the Nicaraguan rainforest below would somehow miraculously disappear, and she'd be back in her apartment again.

And when it didn't for the umpteenth time, she did the next best thing. She berated him for it.

Again.

"So, what? You couldn't get me to go out with you under normal circumstances, so you arranged all this?" She spread her arms wide. "Well, joke's on you, buddy, because I don't even like being in nature. What on earth were you even thinking? I–"

"Actually, this was my doing."

She spun towards the sound of the voice that had spoken and lost her breath because before her stood someone she could only describe as the heaven-sent embodiment of one of her most treasured fantasies. Six foot five at least. Dark. Gorgeous. Like Aaron Pierre gorgeous. And buff. Built like a South Korean, Black Panther battle tank.

On steroids.

Only with crystal clear, luminous blue eyes, and way more beautiful…and wearing… jeans?

"Mel. Trent." He nodded at each of them in turn. "Just the two people I needed to see. I'm Raphael, and oh…have I got a message for you."

He crossed powerful arms over his massive chest and grinned.

Did you catch the other books in the series?
<u>Surrender</u>
<u>Transform</u>
<u>Delight</u>
<u>Verndari Awakening</u>

Love is Deborah Lamoreaux's raison d'être.

She lives to immerse her readers in a rich fantasy world where magical faraway places and unwavering fated love all come together to create a delicious, satisfying melting pot of literary distraction.

In her world love is always true, unexpected, undeniable, unconditional and of course… everlasting.

Ms. Lamoreaux only ever comes alive when she's let loose to produce her next work of romantic fiction and each and every time that you journey alongside her, within the pages of one of her creations, she escapes the confines of imagination…
So come, escape with her…

Sign up for Forget Me Not Romances <u>newsletter</u> and receive a special gift compiled from Forget Me Not Authors!